WHISKEY BUSINESS

A MIXOLOGY LOUNGE MYSTERY

ADRIAN ANDOVER

Chestnut
Avenue
Press

eBook ISBN: 979-8-9985692-0-3

Paperback ISBN: 979-8-9985692-1-0

Cover Design: Dawn Adams, DA Cover Designs

For all of my parents—
Mom and Lynn; Dad and Cathi

I'm so grateful I grew up in homes where you all read so voraciously.
Because you read, I read.
Because I read, I write.

ONE

I rested my blowtorch on the bar. "I need tonight to go off without a hitch." The scent of toasted marshmallow delighted my nostrils as I garnished the s'mores cocktail I was perfecting.

"It will, Reece. What could go wrong?" Ava, my fellow mixologist and employee, placed her empty cocktail shaker on the bar. "We're not even officially open tonight."

I scratched at my stubbled jawline and let out a small chuckle. "You're right. I just want everything to be perfect. It'll be a great opportunity to showcase the lounge."

Soon, the Lifted Spirits whiskey club would be hosting its monthly tasting in Subplot, my literary-themed cocktail lounge located in the basement of D'Amico's Italian restaurant.

"They're going to love it." She gestured an open hand at the cozy scene in front of us. "How could they not?"

Eclectic neon library chic was the vibe I aimed for when designing Subplot. Built-in bookshelves lined the windowless walls, and understated color-changing lights bordered the ceiling. An assortment of mismatched seating, including brown leather reading chairs and mid-century velvet couches, flanked coffee tables throughout the lounge. Desk lamps with green glass lampshades at each table conveyed a traditional library ambience. On Thursday through Sunday nights, when we were open to the public, we dimmed the lights to a soft orange glow, making the lounge feel like a comfy study in an old noir film.

We returned to crafting drinks for our summer menu, which was set to launch a few weeks later, under fluorescent tube lights hanging from the ceiling, which we only turned on outside of business hours.

As I drizzled a thin chocolate ganache over the golden marshmallow and dusted it with crumbs from our house-made graham crackers, my mind inevitably drifted back to Chloe.

Breaking her heart was never part of my plan. But after years of coming to terms with being gay, I broke off our engagement six months before our wedding day, leaving her heart understandably broken.

Amidst my endless guilt and sleepless nights, I dealt with my feelings the way we always did in the Parker family—by distracting myself with hard work.

After the breakup, I wasted no time getting to work on opening Subplot in my charming hometown of Hope Mills, Pennsylvania. Growing up, I'd always looked up to my father, Frank Parker, who was a renowned bartender and mixologist in his own right. From the time I was old enough to hold a job at fourteen, I'd worked in fine dining restaurants around town and in bars since I'd turned twenty-one. In the ten years since, I'd dreamed about opening a cocktail lounge which combined my love of reading and mixology, and I finally brought my vision to life.

Between securing a business loan and liquor license, renting, furnishing, and renovating a space, hiring a team, and working diligently to become profitable as soon as possible, I didn't have room in my life for romance.

And that was just fine by me.

Despite my wonderful years with Chloe, the broken engagement taught me I didn't know much about relationships.

I barely even knew who I was.

"Where did the grenadine sneak off to?" Ava searched through the bottles in the step shelf behind the bar to my left where we stored our bitters and syrups.

"Grenadine?" I blinked myself back to the present moment.

She bobbed her head with a smile.

"Oh, yeah. Right. It's over ..." I dragged out the words as my hand surfed above the bottles in front of me. "Here!" I picked up the bottle of the deep red bar syrup, which I'd made fresh the day before from pomegranate juice, lemon juice, and sugar, and handed it to her.

A hard, rhythmic knock pounded on our downstairs exit, jostling liquor bottles and further freeing me from my shameful internal monologue. I put down the cocktail shaker and jogged past Ava and around the bar to see who was there.

There were two ways to get in and out of Subplot—through an average metal door downstairs which led to an alley, and through a secret bookcase in the vestibule of D'Amico's restaurant upstairs. Most customers used the latter, which also served as a Little Free Library.

"Special delivery," a familiar gruff voice announced. When I pushed the door open, the familiar figure of a man in cowboy boots, jeans, a cream-colored T-shirt, and long blond locks tucked under a backward trucker hat came into view. He held a cardboard box under one arm.

"Hey, Logan. How's it going, man?" I reached out my colorful sleeve-tattooed arm for a handshake, and he clapped his free hand firmly with mine.

Although he looked like a country music star, Logan Nelson was the founder and owner of one of our main suppliers: Delaware Crossing Distilling Company, often abbreviated to

DCDC by locals. The name alluded to George Washington crossing the Delaware River on Christmas night in 1776. That historic American Revolutionary War moment took place a few miles south of Hope Mills, and the town's colonial American roots were still on proud display. In addition to producing and distributing liquor locally, DCDC also educated visitors on the history of liquor and the distilling process.

"I'm doing well, my dude. I have a few bottles of our new double-barrel bourbon. Will Kaufman ordered these for tonight's tasting."

Will was the president of the longstanding Lifted Spirits whiskey club. On the second Wednesday of each month, they got together to taste whiskey, socialize, experiment with food pairings, and learn about the craft of distilling from experts in the field. They'd been meeting in various locations around town, but now that Subplot was opened, they planned to make it their headquarters.

Wednesdays had proven to be slow, so we weren't officially open for business, but I was happy to offer up my space for tastings one Wednesday evening a month. It served as an opportunity to promote my lounge to people who appreciated the craft of liquor and insights into the magical world of mixology.

Plus, I'd never balk at a chance to earn some additional income for my new business. With Subplot still in its infancy, every interaction laid the groundwork for building a loyal customer base. I needed the evening's Lifted Spirits club to go off without a hitch, as it was a great opportunity to attract new regulars.

I squinted at Logan as the sun hung low in the sky, getting ready to set. "Are you hanging around for the meeting? The club should be arriving any minute now."

"I was planning on it." He rubbed his palms together. "I can't wait to hear what everyone thinks of the new bourbon."

I stepped out into the cool evening air to hold the door open, and Logan carried the box inside. He took a seat at the bar and chatted with Ava as we made the final preparations before the tasting.

About five minutes later, the upstairs doorbell buzzed through the vacant lounge.

"That must be the first from the club," I called out to Ava, who was behind the bar as I fluffed pillows in the seating area.

"I'll hit the lights," she responded before flipping off the fluorescent rods one-by-one, plunging the room into a soft amber glow.

She was always one step ahead of me. As colleagues, we just clicked, a product of our years working together at another bar. When I opened Subplot, I knew she'd be the perfect fit to bring my vision to life, and she was the first person I called to join my team. Thank goodness she'd said yes.

As my eyes adjusted to the dim light, I hustled around the bar, through the seating area, and up the two flights of stairs to open the unassuming door that backed the secret bookcase.

On any other evening, Lainey, our maître d', would be stationed next to it to welcome guests on a first-come, first-served basis, check IDs, manage our waitlist when needed, and escort guests downstairs to their tables. Since she didn't work on Wednesdays, I propped the bookcase door open so other members could find their way down to the lounge.

A bright yellow sticky note on the podium caught my eye. I peeled it off. *The bookshelf is looking a bit unkempt.* It was yet another passive-aggressive note from my upstairs neighbor Heidi, the owner of D'Amico's. Though customers often shared that the bookshelf added charm to our shared vestibule, she constantly found reasons to complain.

The first guests, a woman with shoulder-length curly blonde hair and a man with short brown curls, both of whom I estimated to be in their mid-thirties, followed me through the secret bookcase as I crumpled the note in my palm.

"Welcome to Subplot!" I exclaimed as they stepped through the passageway behind me.

"Wow!" they both marveled as they stepped further down the staircase.

A white neon sign which spelled NOW ENTERING WONDER-LAND in giant cursive letters welcomed guests at the bottom of the first landing before the staircase turned to lead them to the underground retreat.

"This space is incredible," the woman commented. "Do you own this place?"

I nodded. "Thank you." I introduced myself and exchanged handshakes with the two members, who shared their names were Kristin and Theo. "If there's anything I can help you with while you're here, give me a holler. Otherwise, this space belongs to the Lifted Spirits tonight."

Kristin and Theo sat at two high-backed leather armchairs near the bar, exchanged pleasantries with Logan, and chatted amongst themselves.

I returned behind the bar to clean up the graham crackers, marshmallows, chocolate ganache drizzle, and dirty barware utensils at my workstation from the experimentation I'd done before Logan arrived. I placed bottles back where they belonged and ensured all the labels faced outward, taking pride in my organized bar.

The hum of conversation grew louder as more members trickled in. Ava meandered through the lounge to offer glasses of water to each person as they sat down.

"I sure hope Mr. Kentucky doesn't ruin tonight's meeting like he did last month," I overheard Kristin say as she placed her glass of water on the end table between her and Theo.

I couldn't help but eavesdrop—partly due to my curiosity,

but mostly because of the way Kristin's loud voice carried in my direction.

I was no stranger to the poor choices people sometimes made once they imbibed. However, my experience with tastings were usually more subdued. Whiskey clubs were typically more interested in the craft and flavor profile of the spirit rather than getting drunk, although the relaxation which accompanied was usually a welcome by-product.

Theo's shoulders rolled with his laughter. "If what we saw upstairs is any indication of how tonight will go, it'll be an interesting meeting for sure. The guy's trashed already."

Kristin tittered, pulling at her dangly earring. "I can't tell if he's sloshed or if acting obnoxious is his M.O."

Theo, dressed in a maroon sweater over a collared shirt, bounced as he laughed. "What's his name again? Brendan? Brant?"

"Brent." Kristin hunched her shoulders and pretended she might be sick after saying his name. "He's so full of himself. It took everything in me to not put him in his place last month. If he says something stupid tonight, I won't be able to keep my cool."

A quick chill tickled my spine at the thought of confrontation. Memories of the handful of fights I'd broken up over the years flashed through my mind. As a conflict-averse person, bar fights surged my adrenaline. Sometimes they got gnarly, but unfortunately, nothing surprised me about the poor choices people sometimes made when they'd had one—or a few—too many drinks.

Theo pumped his fist. "Yeah, you show him."

Please don't. I needed tonight to be smooth and successful. If it wasn't, I feared it might create a negative association with Subplot and scare away potentially loyal customers.

Kristin sat forward in her chair and puffed out her chest.

"'Look at me, I'm Brent,'" she mocked with a deep, Southern-accented voice. "'I'm from Kentucky, the whiskey capital of the world, and I know more than all you idiots. *Blah, blah, blah.*'"

Kristin and Theo both erupted into laughter, garnering chuckles from other club members seated near them.

"I've never met such a loudmouth know-it-all in all my life, and that's saying something," she said.

A man I recognized as Will, the club's president, stepped toward them with three cardboard boxes balanced between his palms and two canvas grocery bags dangling from one arm. He had clean-cut salt-and-pepper hair and wore a blue dress shirt, gray suit pants and matching sportscoat, and black wingtip dress shoes. We'd already met once when he stopped by the lounge a couple of weeks before to ask about hosting his club at Subplot, but I also recognized him from the signs around town promoting his financial advising business. Though he wasn't in the whiskey business by trade, he had a passion for the craft and enjoyment of the spirit, even going on trips to taste whiskey around the world.

"Aw, come on, you two." Will spoke in a calm, hushed tone, making it difficult to make out every word, but I caught the gist. "I know our new member can be—"

"A real jerk?" Kristin blurted out as Will stumbled to find the right words.

"No," Will cocked his head to the side. "He has a ... different approach. That's all. Can you please keep it down? I don't want anyone to get the wrong idea about our club. This is meant to be an inclusive space."

"Fine," Kristin huffed. "But if he gets out of line tonight, I *will* say something. Being an inclusive club doesn't mean we give Brent license to be narcissistic and condescending. I'll actually *do* something about it if he's disrespectful. It isn't fair to the rest of us."

Will released a heavy sigh. I got the sense he was frustrated with Kristin, but too much of a peacekeeper to entirely stand his ground.

Will pivoted to greet Logan at the bar before he approached me. I quickly looked away and pretended to straighten up bottles.

"Reece—how've you been?" I got the sense Will was in a networking mindset, always schmoozing and trying to build relationships with potential clients. As a new business owner, I was fresh meat.

"I'm doing great," I answered, referring strictly to my professional life. "How about you?"

"Good, good." He held out the stacked boxes in my direction. "I picked up some pecan pies from Jackie and Jill's Bakery to pair with tonight's tasting. And I brought some plates and utensils as well. Do you mind if I lay these out here?"

I spread both arms out in front of me, gesturing at the empty bar, beside the DCDC bourbon bottles positioned in the center. "Go right ahead. Make yourself at home."

"You and your staff aren't allergic, are you?"

I shook my head. "I'm not."

"Me either," Ava chimed in as she scurried behind the bar to refill the water pitcher. "Sorry to eavesdrop, Will. I heard pecan pie and my ears perked right up. It's my favorite. I know it's six months away, but I'd venture to say it's the ultimate Thanksgiving pie."

"Whoa, whoa, whoa," I barked. "What about pumpkin?"

Ava and Will glanced at one another and simultaneously grimaced at me.

"Yeah, sorry. Pecan is where it's at," Will said, prompting an approving wink from Ava.

"I'm on your side, dude," Logan chimed in.

"I'm glad someone has my back," I teased.

The lounge filled up over the next ten minutes, and it bustled with the low rumble of conversation until a man wearing a red-checkered flannel shirt, faded jeans, and motorcycle boots clomped down the bottom flight of stairs into the lounge, each step heavier and slower than the one before.

As he stepped further into the seating area, a silence fell over the group's twenty or so members, except for a few nervous whispers. Most of them turned to face the man while the others exchanged awkward glances.

Was this the man Kristin and Theo mocked several minutes before?

I squinted through the dim light at Kristin, who sat in the same leather chair near the bar. She turned in my direction to face Theo, placing a hand on the side of her mouth to shield her lips from being read by the rest of the group, although she mumbled just loud enough for me to hear. "Here we go again."

TWO

"Hi, Brent. We're glad you're able to join us for this month's meeting." Will's deep, warm voice broke the silence that pervaded the cocktail lounge.

Members of Lifted Spirits gave disapproving looks at one another as if to ask, *Did he say we?*

Will gestured his arm toward an empty chair at one of the tables near the bar. "There's an open seat right over here. Make yourself comfortable."

The other members seated at the table shifted in their chairs.

Brent squinted at Will, then plodded toward them with his shoulders pushed back and lips tight. His heavy footsteps and a few faint whispers were the only sounds in the room. He slunk down into the seat.

Will, the sole standing member of the club, clapped his hands once and rubbed them together as he spoke. "Alright, I'd say we have enough folks here to kick things off. It's hard to believe we're already having our May meeting. It's great to see a few new faces, too. And this month, we're especially grateful

Subplot has agreed to host our group. Isn't this space amazing?"

"Is a musty basement the best you could do?" Brent interrupted.

Did my lounge actually smell musty?

I couldn't keep a shocked chuckle from escaping my mouth. Sure, Subplot was in a basement, but cleanliness was a top priority, and my contractor-slash-best friend Nate had helped me completely remodel the space.

Kristin sat so far forward in her chair she practically hovered over it.

"Can we get to the tasting already?" Brent slid his butt back on his chair and leaned forward, resting both elbows on his knees, hands dangling in front of him. "It's a whiskey club meeting, not the United Nations. Do you have to be so formal?"

Will's eyes widened at the interjection and placed a hand over his chest.

I ran my fingers over my short, almost buzz-cut hair. This was a disaster. So much for a smooth evening. I hoped the rift between the club's members wouldn't escalate any further.

Kristin growled under her breath. "Be quiet."

Will pressed down on the air beside him with one hand, signaling for Brent to calm down before addressing him on the other side of the room. "I usually kick off our meetings each month with some brief remarks and updates. Our members all pay dues so we can bring in experts to speak and to cover the food and beverage we enjoy, so I like to keep everyone informed with what's going on."

Brent scoffed. "Fine. Do whatever makes you feel important."

His rude comments shocked me. Why would he pay dues to belong to a club he disapproved of so strongly?

After sharing a few updates about the club, Will transitioned to introducing the evening's tasting. "Tonight, we'll be enjoying a brand new double-barrel bourbon, distilled right here in town by Delaware Crossing Distilling Company. We're also lucky to have Logan Nelson from DCDC here tonight." He opened an arm toward Logan, who was still seated at the bar.

Logan rose and stood next to Will as he waved at the group. "We just launched this bourbon a couple of weeks ago, so I'm excited to hear what you all think of it. I'm all ears for feedback so we can make improvements on future batches."

"Would you mind sharing some background on this bourbon with all of us?" Will asked.

"Sure, man. I know I'm in the presence of some whiskey connoisseurs"—Logan's symmetrical smile beamed as he spoke —"so you might already know this, but I'll give you some background just in case you didn't. The term *double-barrel* means we first aged the whiskey in a charred oak barrel before transferring it to another barrel to mature further. At DCDC, we actually used gin barrels for the second round of aging, which hopefully contributes some smoothness. When you taste, look for some notes of vanilla, oak, and caramel, which also come from that second barrel."

I was impressed with Logan's knowledge and how eloquently he shared it with the group, eliciting nods from members.

"It's a shame we have to taste this knock-off bourbon," Brent interrupted again, causing a few gasps and whispering chatter from the group.

Logan raised his eyebrows, pressed his lips together, and took a step back toward the bar. He didn't respond.

It wasn't my place to speak up, but I found it difficult to keep my mouth shut, especially given my passion for local distilling and Brent's earlier jab at my lounge. Plus, I felt a duty to stand up for my fellow small business owner. "Just because this whiskey is distilled locally doesn't mean it's any lower quality. I've gotten to know Logan and took a tour through his process. You should check it out sometime. He goes great lengths to ensure his spirits are of the highest quality. It's quite impressive, actually." Hopefully, I didn't sound like too much of a know-it-all, myself.

Theo sat up in his chair. "I've taken the tour, too. It's free and open to the public, and I highly recommend it."

"That's cute." Brent forced an exaggerated smile and sprung up to his feet. "You people wouldn't know the first thing about real, quality whiskey if you were drowning in it. I'm from Kentucky where we do whiskey right."

Theo's leg bounced uncontrollably in his seat.

Kristin popped up from her chair and rushed over to Will. "See, I told you. Make him leave," she hissed through clenched teeth.

Brent's boots clacked on the concrete floor as he approached Will and Kristin. "If we all end up getting sick or going blind or worse"—Brent dragged an index finger in front of his throat and stuck out his tongue with closed eyes— "it'll be because I drank *this* cheap whiskey."

Logan huffed and shook his head. I couldn't tell if he was disappointed or upset, but if I'd been in his position, I don't know that I could have sat there silently.

I glanced at Ava, pulling the corners of my lips down into a winced grimace. Did I need to kick Brent out? Though I considered it, I also didn't want to overstep Will's leadership in front of all his club members.

She shrugged with a dumbfounded expression.

"Alright, that's enough." Will's thunderous voice cut through Brent and Kristin's overlapping jabs, finally hushing them both. "Could you both *please* sit down? We're supposed to be having fun here." He looked from Brent to Kristin.

They both complied, returning to their respective seats without argument, although Brent did so with an eyeroll.

Will pointed at me over his shoulder with his right thumb. "Reece back here—the owner of this fine establishment—is right. Even though the bourbon we're about to taste was produced down the street, Logan has studied the craft extensively." Will lowered his pointed thumb and panned an open hand toward Brent. "Kentucky *is* renowned as one of the greatest whiskey regions in the world, and Logan has gone there many times to study and learn from some of the greatest distillers on the planet."

Logan pressed his hands together and bowed his thanks to Will.

Will cleared his throat. "The warm, almost spicy flavor of the bourbon pairs wonderfully with sweet desserts like pecan pie. The sweetness of the pie is the perfect balance to the big-bodied flavor of the bourbon. And both the whiskey and pie share flavors of vanilla and spices, so they make the perfect pair."

He spun around and asked me, "Is it okay if I come behind the bar to serve up this pie?"

"Sure thing." I gave a tight nod to Ava beside me, hoping the evening's drama was behind us.

Will turned to Logan. "Do you want to do the honors of serving the bourbon?"

Logan nodded and joined Ava and me behind the bar.

Will turned to address the room. "Alright. We're ready to begin our tasting. I can't wait to hear what you all think of this pairing. If you could line up at the bar, we'll take care of you."

As members approached the bar, Will served them a slice of pecan pie on a brown compostable paper plate with a black plastic fork and a bar napkin. From there, they shuffled to the side to collect their glass of whiskey.

Ava handed me two glasses at a time, and I lined them up on the bar, shifting them toward Logan as he poured each serving and handed them off to members.

We served the bourbon in snifter glasses, which resembled wine glasses, although smaller and with shorter stems, wider bottoms, and narrower rims. Most folks chose to drink their whiskey on its own—or neat—during tastings. Others preferred to taste it on the rocks or with drops of water to enhance the spirit's subtle flavors, so we had a bucket of ice with tongs and a small glass dropper bottle filled with water available on the bar.

When it was Kristin's turn to pick up her slice of pie and whiskey, she substituted her thanks with an apology on behalf of the entire Lifted Spirits group. "Sorry you've had to deal with all of our drama." She rolled her eyes and let out an annoyed chuckle. "It's not usually like this, but some people don't know how to conduct themselves, am I right?"

Will turned his head in our direction before folding his arms and looking down at the bar, shaking his head disapprovingly.

I gave her an awkward smile and nodded. "No apologies needed whatsoever. I'm glad to be hosting you all. I hope my basement will do." I hated to feed into Kristin's pointed comment and my insecurity following Brent's remark, but I couldn't resist making a small quip.

"Are you kidding? It's amazing down here!" Kristin reassured me.

"Truly," Will added. "You've got a good thing going."

As the line dwindled down to the last two members, Brent stood up from his seat and marched over to the bar with hands on his hips, planting his heel firmly on the ground with each step.

"Looks like I almost planned it perfectly," Will told Brent

with a smirk. "I have two slices left. And here I thought I didn't order enough."

Brent grunted, snatched the plate of pie from Will, and picked up a glass of whiskey without acknowledging me or Ava. He sidestepped further down the bar and added a couple of drops of water to his glass—the only club member who'd done so, as far as I'd witnessed.

Will glanced over at us. "I'm sorry I don't have enough for both of you. I wish I had grabbed another pie. Feel free to duke it out for the last slice."

Ava and I each waved him off as if to say, *That's perfectly fine. Don't worry about it.*

Will shrugged. "Alright, if you insist." He plated the final slice for himself.

The lounge rumbled with conversation until Will spoke up, using his strong voice to gather everyone's attention. "Alright, since everyone's been served, I recommend first taking a sip of your whiskey and discussing before you try the pie pairing. Thank you all for coming tonight, and let's all give a toast to summer kicking off in a few weeks."

Around the lounge, every member raised their glass before gently clinking them with their surrounding neighbors.

Except for Brent, of course. He didn't interact with anyone during the toast. Instead, he devoured his slice of pie and barely sniffed his bourbon.

"That's it?" he hollered out to no one in particular from his slouched position in his chair with one leg dangling over his other knee. "I thought this was supposed to be a serious, *real* whiskey club. All you people do is eat pie, drink, and talk?" A bitter laugh escaped from his mouth. "What about the craft? What about the ritual?"

Minutes before, Brent criticized Will for being too formal. His comments about the club not being serious enough showed he was perpetually petty. Some people thrived on having something to be upset about.

"That's *enough!*" Kristin's loud voice screeched through the lounge like an angry cat. Turning my attention toward the yell, her curly blonde hair bounced as she stomped over to Brent. "Out! Out!"

Brent surveyed his glass, which he still hadn't taken a sip from.

"You've been nothing but rude since the moment you stepped in here," she continued. "If you hate this club so much and are going to disrespect literally all of us, why don't you leave?"

Theo clasped his hand around Kristin's shoulder, coaxing her back to where they'd been sitting.

Brent pushed himself up to his feet. "I paid my dues here, ya know. I have every right to be here." He took out his worn black leather wallet. "I've got my membership card right here, if you don't believe me."

Did Lifted Spirits actually issue cards, or was he being snarky?

"I'll gladly refund your dues—out of my own pocket, if I have to—if it means you'll never come back again," she said.

Whispers from the club's members grew louder. Many of them sat up in their seats, some even calling out for him to sit down, be quiet, or leave.

Once again, Will tried to gain control of the room, gesturing for everyone to calm down.

"Whatever happened to 'everyone is welcome here?'" Brent mocked with exaggerated hand gestures and a high-pitched voice before strutting toward the lounge's downstairs exit to the alley.

At the threshold, he spun around. "I'm done with you all. You're all dead to me," he yelled, panning his index finger from one side of the lounge to the other to signal he meant *everyone.* "Enjoy your tasting."

"Wait!" I called out from my position behind the bar. "You can't leave with that." I pointed at the glass in his hand. "That's an open container."

He punched the crash bar on the exit door and allowed it to slam behind him as he stormed out of the meeting with his drink still in hand.

Kristin let out an irritated groan.

I hurried over to the door to try and keep Brent from running off with the glass. I stepped out into the alley, but Brent was nowhere to be seen.

Shoot. I better not lose my liquor license over this.

I went back inside and closed the door gently behind me as the chatter between the Lifted Spirits members grew louder.

"I'm so sorry about that, everyone." Will's booming voice projected through the crowd once again.

The cocktail lounge faded from uproarious conversation to silence in a split second.

Will sighed. "Can we all take a deep breath, have another sip, and try to relax?"

He sucked in a deep breath, lifting his free hand over his chest to lead the group. The collective deep breath of approximately two dozen people swelled through the basement as they inhaled, held their breath for a few seconds, and exhaled. I followed along and found some semblance of relief after dealing with such a difficult personality.

Luckily, the tasting resumed, and peace returned to Subplot. Many of the club members lined up for a second serving, and I was glad to overhear chatter about carpooling and designated drivers.

Ava took a lap around the lounge to collect plates, utensils, and glasses from those who'd finished their tasting.

"Ava, why don't you call it a night? It's been an intense evening, and I have everything under control," I told her after she placed the first batch of used snifters in a dirty dishes bin behind the bar.

She cocked her head to the side. "Are you sure? Don't you need help cleaning up and doing dishes?"

"Don't worry about it. The hard work is done. I can handle the rest."

Logan readjusted his backward hat. "I think it's about that time for me, too."

He departed first. Ava didn't leave long after, only swinging by the office to collect her personal belongings before heading out.

After she left, I refilled the water pitcher and floated around the lounge to serve some hydration to the members before they ventured home. Within a half an hour of her departure, small groups gradually trickled up the staircase to D'Amico's until only Will and I remained.

"I am *so* sorry for what unfolded here tonight." Will massaged his forehead with one hand. "That was *not* par for the course for Lifted Spirits. I can only hope you'll invite us back next month, but I can understand if you're hesitant."

"No worries. I appreciate you going the extra mile to try and defuse the situation. You and the club are all welcome back at Subplot anytime." I pressed the palms of my hands together to try and show Will I was sincere, although I hoped Brent meant it when he said the club was dead to him.

As Will departed, the hard soles of his dress shoes clacked slowly up each step until the secret bookcase door opened and clicked shut.

Once I was alone, I let out a heavy sigh and rubbed my temples in slow circles.

I connected my phone to a Bluetooth speaker behind the

bar and cranked up a playlist of my favorite nineties music, a flashback to riding in the backseat of my mom's car when she drove me to school—a phase of musical taste I'd never grow out of. Sheryl Crow's "All I Wanna Do" filled the empty lounge.

I couldn't help but dance my way up the steps to the upbeat song as I locked our main entrance and back down the stairs as I closed up shop.

I collected all the used snifter glasses, wiped down all the tables and chairs, straightened up furniture in the seating area, loaded the glassware and utensils into the dishwasher, and quickly swept the concrete floor.

Before I stepped out through the downstairs exit to lock up for the night around ten-thirty, I collected a full bag of trash to take out to the dumpster.

Standing beside the door, I surveyed my cocktail lounge, admiring what'd been nothing more than an empty basement and a dream several months before.

I inhaled a deep whiff of air through my nostrils. "Nah. It's not musty down here," I mumbled aloud to no one.

I switched off the lights, disconnected my phone from the speaker midway through Alanis Morissette's "You Learn," and stepped out into the cool spring air, which carried the faint scent of lilacs. It was perfect sleeping-with-the-windows-open weather.

The metal door slammed shut behind me. I locked it, tugged its handle to make sure it was secured, and walked through the dark alley behind Subplot with the bag of trash in hand, faintly illuminated by the orange glow of the streetlights which spilled in from the front side of the building.

My eyes were fixed on the dumpster at the end of the alley. Before I reached it, I tripped, but luckily regained my balance quickly.

At first, I thought I'd stumbled over a fallen branch from one of the many trees clustered behind the lounge. But as I gazed down to see what'd caught my foot, I was dumbfounded.

Is that ... an arm?

I blinked hard, trying to come up with alternatives for what I was looking at.

My breath lurched.

Though it was dark, I could tell the arm was clad in a red-and-black flannel shirt. As I panned my vision up the arm and across the body it was connected to, I was horrified to recognize the blue jeans and motorcycle boots.

I'd tripped over Brent's limp body.

"Brent?" I called before crouching down to the ground, abandoning the bag of garbage at my side. "Brent!" I put my hand on his torso and nudged him, immediately turning my head in the opposite direction to avoid seeing his face.

He didn't respond to my jostling.

With a deep breath, I mustered the courage to look at his face, though it was shrouded in darkness, for any sign of life.

As I tried to wake him up, a sinking awareness washed over me. *He might be more than passed out.*

I placed two fingers on the top of his neck, just under his jaw. *You're being ridiculous, Reece. He probably had too much to drink.*

His skin was cold and stiff to the touch.

He didn't have a pulse.

An empty snifter glass laid in the gravel beside him.

Oh, no. This can't be happening.

I didn't need confirmation from a coroner to know Brent was dead.

THREE

A man passed out behind a cocktail lounge. More than passed out. Dead.

My mind raced with worst case scenarios. The police were going to think I overserved him. And just wait until they found out what happened here tonight. I held the sides of my head. *If it looks like a duck and quacks like a duck.* And once the medical examiner performed an autopsy, what if they found his blood alcohol content was through the roof?

We don't know that for sure yet. For all I knew, Brent could have had a medical emergency. Beyond Kristin and Theo's gossiping, I had no reason to believe he'd had anything to drink other than the single serving of bourbon from the tasting, if he even drank it at all.

Regardless of my fear that my discovery wouldn't end well for me, I needed to call 911 ASAP.

To make a horrible situation worse, one of the officers on our town's small police force was Chloe's brother, Cameron. Cam had been like a brother to me, but I hadn't seen him since I'd ended the engagement.

If he responds, this is going to be awkward.

I slid my phone from the front pocket of my jeans and dialed 911.

"My name is Reece Parker, and I'm in the alley behind D'Amico's Italian Restaurant on Main Street. I was taking out the trash from my cocktail lounge downstairs, and I tripped over a body back here." As soon as I spoke the words, I couldn't believe they flowed out of my mouth so naturally, so pragmatically. Perhaps I was in crisis mode. "At first, I thought he was passed out, but"—I swallowed the lump forming in my throat —"he's dead. I checked for a pulse, but I couldn't feel anything. He's cold."

The dispatcher instructed me to stay on the line while I waited for first responders to arrive on the scene.

It wasn't more than two minutes before the wailing siren of an ambulance sounded in the distance, the urgent shriek and roaring engine growing louder as it approached. In our small town, help was luckily never too far away. A police SUV rolled into the alley shortly after the ambulance arrived.

"Sir, please step away from the body," one of the EMTs yelled at me as they dashed out of the ambulance and rushed over to Brent.

As I backed away, the faint outline of a male police officer hurried toward me.

Everything was washed in an ever-changing red, white, and blue light, making it difficult to make out any other colors.

Please don't be Cam. Please don't be Cam.

"Reece?" the police officer asked in disbelief. "Is that you?"

Yep, it was Cam. I nodded. *Just my luck.*

"Are you okay?" he asked.

I was almost too breathless to respond, but I forced out the words. "Yeah, I'm fine. But I found ..." I pointed toward Brent as if the ambulance and crew of first responders didn't make it obvious why I'd called the police.

"Reece, stay calm. I'm going to talk to the medical team quickly. Please stay right there."

After speaking with the EMTs down the alley, Cam strode slowly back toward me. As he did, he spoke into the shoulder radio strapped over his vest, asking for backup.

"Did they mention what could've happened to him?" I asked when he reached me.

Cam clasped his hands together. "We can't be positive, but the EMTs couldn't attempt resuscitation. Based on the condition of the body, he's been deceased for approximately an hour."

"An hour? Do they think he might have had some type of medical emergency?"

He sucked in an uncomfortable breath. "We'll need an autopsy to confirm, but I believe drugs, or even poisoning due to an overdose, could be responsible."

My mind felt like a car engine failing to fire. "Poisoning?"

"Between the bluish tinge around his lips and the way it appears the deceased groggily laid himself down, I wouldn't be shocked if the toxicology reports reveal some sort of sedative in his system. And if he already had alcohol to drink—"

"Sedative?" I split my eye contact between Cam's shadowy face and the ambulance scene behind him.

He nodded. "He didn't appear to be toppled over, and the medics didn't observe any obvious signs of trauma. Plus, there was an empty glass beside him. We'll need to test that as well."

My stomach dropped as I replayed the evening's events in my mind. There was no way they'd find a potentially lethal substance in the glass. Or was there?

"He also didn't have any form of ID on him, which seems odd," Cam said.

"He didn't? He was at a whiskey tasting in my lounge tonight, and I saw him pull out his wallet."

"I didn't find it on him during my quick search."

"Could he have been robbed?" The wheels in my mind turned on overdrive. "And earlier you mentioned poison. Poison would mean this could have been done ... intentionally."

Cam rocked on his heels. "Unfortunately, it seems like it might be the case. 'The dose makes the poison,' as they say in toxicology. We'll need to secure this area as a crime scene so we can collect evidence, and we need to treat this situation as a homicide. One of my colleagues will be arriving any second to take a statement from you.

Homicide? Murder didn't happen in our quaint, artsy town.

Another SUV peeled into the alleyway. The silhouette of a woman wearing a pant suit and a blouse trotted over to the two of us.

Cam gestured to the woman with shoulder-length brunette hair, who I estimated to be in her late forties. "Reece, this is Detective Joanne Sharp."

"I'm going to need your full name, sir." The skeptical look on her face intimidated me. Did she suspect I had something to do with Brent's death before I'd spoken a word to her?

"Reece Parker."

"Do you have your ID on you?" she asked.

I fished the wallet from my back pocket and handed over my driver's license for her to inspect. As I did so, I couldn't help but wonder what had happened to Brent's wallet in the couple of hours between storming out of Subplot and me finding his body.

This couldn't be good. Subplot's reputation would be doomed once the news got out.

I knew I was getting ahead of myself, but it was difficult to keep from spiraling.

She returned my ID and pulled a small field notebook and pen from her pocket. She flipped it open, ready to jot notes.

"Could you please explain to me exactly how you found this body?"

I explained how I'd locked up the lounge and stumbled over Brent's arm as I took out the trash on my way home for the evening.

The detective motioned over her shoulder at the body behind her. "And do you know who this man is?"

"I believe his name is—was—Brent."

"So, you know him?"

"Oh, no ..." I folded my arms as if it might help me resist Detective Sharp's line of questioning. "No, I don't *know* him. Just his name. Tonight was the first time I ever saw him or knew he existed."

"Continue."

I wasn't about to take her bait. "Continue with what?" I asked, not trying to be difficult—only trying to share the most pertinent information. I planned to answer her questions, not share an entire account which might burden me with undue suspicion.

"In what circumstances did you see this man tonight?" she asked forcefully.

Cam swayed ever so slightly. I wondered if he was nervous for me. Though we had a great relationship while Chloe and I were together, I wasn't sure if he'd be willing to go to bat for me now, since I broke his little sister's heart.

"I'm the owner of a new cocktail bar called Subplot. It's located here, in the basement of D'Amico's. Tonight, we hosted a whiskey club—it's called Lifted Spirits—for a tasting, and he" —I pointed toward the body—"was one of the members at the meeting."

"Hmm ..." the detective grumbled. "And how do you know his name?"

"Some members of the whiskey club said it."

"And how many people were at the meeting?"

I swallowed hard. "Around twenty, maybe? Give or take."

"So out of everyone there, you remembered *his* name, specifically? Why?" Detective Sharp rubbed her chin.

Ooh, she's good.

Before I had a chance to respond, she continued. "Was there anything out of the ordinary about how this man interacted with others at the meeting?"

Where do I even begin?

I considered my next words carefully, not wanting to implicate myself or anyone else unworthy of blame. "I would say he acted pretty … aggressive. He criticized the club and the way it's run."

I answered some more of the detective and Cam's follow-up questions, explaining how Brent interrupted the meeting and eventually stormed out after yelling at the whole room.

"He ran out of the meeting and took his glass with him. His sample was still inside. I warned him about leaving with an open container and chased after him, but he was nowhere to be seen." He couldn't have wandered very far.

Detective Sharp jotted a note and arched a single eyebrow like all the TV detectives do—as if it was a requirement for the job. "I imagine the members of the club didn't take his criticism very well?"

"Honestly …" I turned my eyes to the sky as I searched for a recollection. "For the most part, everyone remained calm."

"And what about the rest?"

I furrowed my brow.

"You said *for the most part* everyone was calm, which makes me believe not everyone *was* calm."

I sighed, not wanting to reveal any specific names. I didn't want my personal perspective and speculations to incriminate anyone else. However, Brent's abrupt death was odd, and Cam had confirmed they needed to proceed as though foul play had been involved. If a cold-blooded killer was on the loose somewhere in Hope Mills, it was in my beloved community's best interest to share as much information as I could.

"There was one member—Kristin, I think. I don't know her last name. She seemed to be very agitated by Brent. When he interrupted the club's president, Will Kaufman, while he spoke, she got irritated and stood up to him."

The detective jotted voraciously in her notebook as if she was sketching a portrait.

After name-dropping both Kristin and Will, I didn't doubt they'd be next in line for questioning. Selfishly, I hoped they wouldn't be upset with me for mentioning their names, but I also had to be transparent if the police suspected something nefarious could've happened. I wanted no share of the blame.

"What did she say to Brent?" Detective Sharp asked without looking up from scribbling notes.

"I can't remember her exact words, but she basically called him out for being rude and acting out of line and told him to leave."

I debated mentioning the remarks she'd made about Brent to Theo before the meeting, but ultimately, I decided against it. It was a stretch to infer Kristin meant murder when she talked about losing her cool or taking action if Brent was disrespectful. When she said she'd *actually do something about it* if Brent acted up, she probably meant standing up to him verbally and nothing more—which was exactly what she'd done. *Right?* This internal deliberation made me more comfortable about not sharing those details with the police.

"Did you witness any other strange interactions between the deceased and anyone else at the meeting?" she asked.

Logan. I didn't want to mention his name—especially because he was my friend, and he hadn't done anything wrong.

But considering how Brent had vilified him during the tasting, I figured it was useful information to share with the detective. I told her about what Brent said about Logan, and she scribbled notes.

"Do you have any reason to believe the victim was overly intoxicated?" she continued.

"Not really."

She arched an eyebrow. "Why do you say that?"

"I can't be one hundred percent sure, but he showed no signs of slurred speech, didn't stumble. He could've had some drinks in him already, but he was coherent, even if he behaved badly."

She twisted her lips to the side as if she wasn't confident in my answer.

"I've been working exclusively in bars for over ten years. I know when it's time to cut somebody off, and Brent didn't concern me." Though he didn't have any issues with balance and spoke clearly, I regretted not stepping in and denying Brent service based on his aggressive behavior alone, whether it indicated intoxication or not.

"And you didn't see or hear anything happening in this alley tonight?" The detective thankfully changed the subject.

"No. There aren't any windows on the back side of this entire building, and I had music playing loudly while I cleaned my lounge. I didn't hear a thing."

Had I not been blasting Sheryl Crow on my speaker as I tidied up, I might've heard a desperate cry for help behind the lounge. What if I could've intervened and called the police before Brent ended up dead? I shivered at the thought.

Detective Sharp squinted as she surveyed the back side of the building. "Do you have any security cameras?"

"I'm afraid not." I deeply regretted not installing any, especially considering the circumstances. When opening the lounge, I figured Hope Mills was generally a safe town with little crime. Starting the business came with a litany of expenses, and security cameras weren't on my immediate list of priorities. I thought they might be a worthwhile investment once I was further down the line and earning more reliable profits.

"I'd like to do a quick walkthrough of the lounge."

"Of course."

I led the detective inside. Unfortunately, I'd already loaded everyone's snifter glasses into the dishwasher, and Will had taken the remaining bottles that'd been purchased for the tasting, so there were no traces left behind to indicate we'd hosted the club at all. Regardless, she searched throughout the lounge, behind the bar, in my office, the restroom, and even our stockroom and small kitchen area. After scoping out Subplot from top to bottom, the only evidence she collected from inside was the dropper bottle Brent had used to cut his whiskey. The trash bag which contained everyone's used plates, forks, and napkins was still in the alley, and I figured the authorities would also gather it as evidence.

"Alright, Mr. Parker, those are all the questions I have for right now. You're free to go home." Her words were like weights being lifted off my chest. "I can't force you to stay in town, but it'd look mighty suspicious if you left, considering the circumstances. Between the way the body was found, the fact the victim consumed alcohol, no knowledge yet on whether he had any health problems, and considering the conflicts you described, we have to take this situation very seriously. Do you understand?"

I nodded, grateful but also trying to appear sincere. "I understand completely. You have my full cooperation, Detective." I pointed toward the flashing ambulance lights. "What's going to happen to Brent?"

Cam peered at the scene behind him before turning back to address me. "We're going to have to tape off the area behind your lounge so our forensics team can complete a more thorough examination. The county coroner should also be arriving soon to collect evidence and begin their investigation. We'll have to complete an autopsy to determine any other injuries, alcohol, substances, or toxins in his system, or other evidence which might help us uncover exactly what happened in this alley tonight. But for now, we need to suspect foul play was involved."

I placed both of my palms on the back of my head, astonished by what I'd stumbled upon and dreading the investigation that was about to unfold.

The detective reached into a pocket inside her blazer and handed me a business card with her direct phone number printed on it. "Please give me a call if you notice anything suspicious around here."

I took the card. "Sure thing."

Above all, I hoped the police didn't view me as a suspect but rather as an innocent community member who came across Brent's body by happenstance.

Not only had Subplot been the ultimate distraction as I navigated my life after Chloe, but it had taken a ton of money to get off the ground. I had a lot of work ahead of me to get Subplot's financials in the positive and repay my small business loans. Any threat to our reputation could be detrimental, and I feared what the negative press surrounding a murder investigation might do.

In addition to ensuring my community remained safe, I was prepared to do almost anything to keep Brent's death from tanking my new business.

FOUR

The next morning, I swung by my parents' house to share my experience from the night before. My parents were both relishing their first year of retirement, and I enjoyed popping in during the day occasionally for a visit.

With spring blossoming into full bloom, my mom, dressed in a T-shirt and pink pajama pants, swept away the layer of dirt and debris that had accumulated over the winter from the front porch. A few weeks from now, she'd be planting marigolds and impatiens in her flowerbeds and hanging baskets of petunias and lobelias on the porch.

She waved and smiled once she spotted me in the driveway. "Well, isn't this a pleasant surprise?" She beamed as she leaned a push broom against the side of the house.

I let out a deep sigh, allowing my entire body to relax as I did. "I wish it was under better circumstances."

She tucked a tuft of her blonde-dyed, shoulder-length hair behind her ear. "Oh, what's wrong?"

I gave her a quick hug after I stepped onto the porch. "I'll explain inside. It's not good. Where's Dad?"

"He's tinkering in the garage."

I chuckled, despite my sullen mood. "I should've figured. He's always tinkering."

"Hey, buddy!" My dad's unmistakable deep voice exclaimed behind me. As a kid, he only called me by my first name when I was in trouble. Otherwise, I was Buddy.

I pivoted and watched as he ambled from the garage's side door and up the front walk to join us. He was dressed in a paint-splattered plaid flannel shirt tucked into a pair of jeans, his gut slightly spilling over his belt.

"How's it going?" He opened his arms for a hug once he climbed the porch steps to stand next to me. After releasing from our embrace, I noticed the crow's feet etched at the corners of his eyes, evidence of the countless smiles he'd enjoyed in his lifetime. His smile could uplift an entire room.

"I've been better. Can we talk inside?"

Stepping into my childhood home always brought back fond memories of running through the house, having NERF wars, and sneaking in and out during my rebellious teenage years—mostly at the encouragement of my friend Nate. While my parents had downsized their belongings and were reno-vating the house room by room—their first major retirement project—some things didn't change, like the cheesy nineties family portraits adorning the walls.

We sat around the dining room table where my parents had been adamant about having *family supper* as often as we could throughout my upbringing, despite my dad's irregular work schedule at his bar and my array of sports and extracurricular activities.

"Reece, tell us what's wrong," my mom said. "Can I get you some water? Or how about a blue Gatorade? You always loved blue Gatorade."

I smiled and accepted, not wanting to be rude. My heart

melted knowing my mom kept the fridge stocked with Gatorade so she could offer it when I visited.

After she returned with the beverage, I stared at the dining table's blond wood. "Someone ... died ... in the alley behind Subplot last night."

My dad's jaw dropped, and my mom's hands flew over her mouth.

"That's terrible!" Her voice was muffled. "Who was it? Do we know them?"

I shook my head. "I don't think so. His name was Brent. Not sure of his last name. He was a member of the whiskey club that held a tasting in the lounge yesterday, and he was there just a couple of hours before I found him."

My dad let out a loud sigh. "*Sheesh* ..." He stared past me.

"You found him?" My mom's voice was shaky.

I bobbed my head. "I stumbled upon the body while I took a load of trash out to the dumpster."

My mom, who could cry at something as simple as the beautiful sight of a hummingbird zipping around the backyard, began to sob and leaned on my dad's shoulder.

"I have no words." My dad scratched at his short gray hair. "I can't imagine how you must be feeling."

"Honestly, I'm a bit numb. I think I'm in shock, and it's not really sinking in even though it's all I can think about. I keep replaying it in my mind."

I explained my arrangement with the whiskey club and summarized the series of events that led to tripping over Brent's limp arm. "And of *course* Chloe's brother Cam was the officer who responded to my call. I hadn't seen him since before—"

"You know, I was just thinking about how this weekend would have been your wedding day." My mom sighed. "I get sad whenever I think about it."

I shouldn't have mentioned Cam.

Ever since I'd ended my engagement, my mom tended to be dramatic any time something even tangentially related to Chloe or the topic of marriage was brought up. In fact, I found myself questioning whether my mom took the news harder than Chloe had.

I didn't respond to her lamentation.

"I still don't understand why. Did Chloe do something?" she asked.

I let out a small, frustrated laugh and shook my head. "She didn't do anything. It's between her and me."

I had yet to tell my parents that I was gay. Between the difficult time they were having with my breakup and my mom's incessant pleas for grandchildren, I wasn't ready to open up about the real reason we broke up.

Though I had no reason to believe my parents were homophobic, I feared coming out because I hated to shatter the illusion of what they'd envisioned for my life. I was still on the path to self-acceptance, and it was difficult to consider that my future wouldn't look anything like I thought it would.

In traditional Parker family fashion, I spoke vaguely, worked hard, and carried on with my life as if everything was okay. Even if it wasn't.

"How did we get to talking about the engagement again?" my dad chimed in. "We were talking about a dead body you found yesterday evening."

"Right. Cam responded to my 911 call. After speaking with the medics and observing the body and scene, he thinks the victim could've been poisoned. They secured the alley behind the lounge as a crime scene, and they need to proceed as though foul play was involved. I was free to leave, but they had to bring in the coroner and a forensics team to begin investigating." I rubbed my eyes as if I might reopen them to a new reality. "This is going to look terrible for Subplot. What if this scares away customers and tanks my business?"

"What should he do, Frank?" My mom gripped my dad's arm as if he was all-knowing.

"Tell the truth." My dad spoke matter-of-factly. "Cooperate with Cam and the other authorities. Mind your business. And do your best with your head held high. It's all you can do."

"Should I close the lounge tonight out of respect? On one hand, it feels like the right thing to do. But on the other, any Thursday I'm not open, I'm losing money. Call me insensitive for saying that, but it's not like I chose for this to happen outside my lounge."

My parents exchanged a glance and then looked away, searching the room for an answer.

"I don't think there's any harm in opening the lounge tonight," my dad said. "You can't help where this happened. And besides, you might hear some gossip that might be valuable for police. You and I both know that some of the biggest secrets are spilled in bars."

Beyond inspiring me to follow in his footsteps as a mixologist, my father was my personal hero, and I trusted him intrinsically.

"And opening tonight won't make me look like a total jerk?"

My dad shook his head. "Not at all. In fact, I think it'd draw more unwanted attention to your lounge if you closed."

"You have a point there."

My mom stood up and walked around the table to hug me from behind. "And you're not a jerk. The fact you're concerned about that shows you care. Just be safe, please."

"I'm so sorry to be the bearer of bad news." I lifted my hand toward my chest to pat my mom's soft hand resting there. Being in her embrace brought back the feeling of safety such gestures brought me as a child. Even as an adult, it felt as if my parents could make everything better.

"Who wants cinnamon rolls?" Mom asked. "I baked them yesterday. I can warm them back up in the oven."

"I can't say no to that," my dad said, as if we hadn't been discussing such a serious topic.

I'd always seen my parents' positivity in tough situations as resilience, but as I grew older, it became clearer that they'd repressed and compartmentalized their emotions rather than dealing with them all along.

Considering how I'd used opening Subplot as a distraction from my breakup, I wondered if I'd inherited the trait from them.

As unresolved as I felt, I ate my mom's warm, gooey cinnamon roll slathered with cream cheese frosting with a smile painted on my face.

FIVE

As I strode down Main Street to Subplot early that afternoon, I tried to enjoy the beautiful spring weather, even though it felt like a storm cloud hovered over me.

Large green leaves dangled over my head from towering maple trees, allowing small patches of sunlight to shine on the brick sidewalk. Baskets of petunias hung from planters on the lampposts, and lush ivy covered some of the colonial brick buildings that formed our historic downtown. The cool breeze was perfect for walking around outside with no jacket, which felt refreshing after a harsh winter and cold, rainy April.

I slipped the phone out of my pocket as I strolled and checked social media for the first time since I'd discovered Brent's body. Sure enough, the first post in my feed was an article with the headline BREAKING NEWS: AUTHORITIES INVESTIGATE SUSPICIOUS DEATH BEHIND LOCAL COCKTAIL LOUNGE.

My heart sunk. *This is going to be a nightmare for business.*

I tapped on the article to see if any new details had come out about Brent's death. Though it unfortunately named Subplot, the story was vague and didn't identify the victim.

After my tragic discovery the night before, I couldn't bear to walk through the alley behind the lounge past yellow police tape. Instead, I decided to enter the speakeasy through the vestibule Subplot shared with D'Amico's as my customers would.

I walked up the restaurant's three wide front steps and pushed open the glass door which led to our communal foyer. Even through the closed main door into the restaurant, the scents of simmering tomato sauce, basil, and fresh-baked bread delighted my senses.

Though it was a long shot, I hoped Heidi, the restaurant's owner, wouldn't see me. I was slightly terrified of her on a good day, which was usually enough to make me avoid using the upstairs entrance altogether. She was uptight and critical of me as a downstairs neighbor, claiming I was stealing business from her and that I invited bad behavior into the building.

Despite my sweaty palms and racing heart, I peered into the restaurant's glass double-doors. Perhaps it was my curious nature, but I hoped to catch a glimpse of how Heidi was handling the news. Was she angry? Frantic? Sad? At two o'clock on a Thursday afternoon, the lunch crowd had filtered out, and it was much too early for the dinner crowd.

I bit my lower lip when I spotted Heidi sitting at a table to the far left of the dining room, her wavy brunette hair cascading flawlessly over each shoulder. Her thick-framed glasses rested low on her nose as she appeared to be deeply focused on her laptop. She covered her mouth with one hand and shook her head as she studied the screen.

While staring through the doors, I drew the attention of one of the waitresses, Ashley, as she wiped down a table inside as if she was in slow motion. She was typically energetic and all smiles, but today she appeared tense.

I gave her a small wave, and she returned the gesture with a slight, forced grin as I turned to unlock the bookcase.

After stepping through it, the heavy door latched shut behind me, and a fleeting relief washed over me.

The tightness in my shoulders relaxed as I hustled down both flights of stairs and past the Now Entering Wonderland sign into the lounge. Despite the previous night's events, being back at Subplot, surrounded by books and my mixology tools, brought me a sense of calm. Being able to disappear into my work—just as I'd done after breaking off the engagement—felt like an escape.

The fluorescent rod lights we used during off-hours were already illuminated, and the rhythmic shaking of ice in a metal cocktail shaker echoed from behind the bar.

"Ava?" I called out from across the room. "You're here early."

Of my three employees—Ava, our maître d' Lainey, and our server Dante—she was the only one who had a key to Subplot. Although I owned the lounge, I viewed her as my equal. We often collaborated and both contributed an equal number of drinks to our menu.

She jolted and gasped, placing the cocktail shaker on the bar and covering her chest with both hands. She breathed deeply and audibly. "You scared me, Reece!"

"You're like" —I checked the time on the silver watch I wore on my left hand— "three hours early for your shift. I didn't realize you'd be here. I'm so sorry I startled you. I tried to be extra stealthy when I opened the door since I was trying to avoid you-know-who upstairs."

Ava let out a chuckle. "You usually come in downstairs, so you caught me off-guard, I guess."

"Sorry about that." I scratched the back of my neck. "I couldn't bear to come in down here after—"

Ava's forehead crinkled. "Yeah, what's up with all the caution tape in the alley?"

I gritted my teeth and sucked in a shallow breath. "You

haven't heard?" Hadn't she searched for an answer online or seen the news on social media?

"No." She let out an uncomfortable titter. "What's going on?"

I pressed a palm to my forehead. "Sorry, I meant to fill you in. Remember that guy from last night—Brent? The one who caused a scene?"

"How could I forget him?"

"His body was found out by the dumpster." My shoulders sunk and I hung my head, not ready to reveal I'd been the one who'd discovered his lifeless body.

Her eyes grew wide. "Found? As in ...? Oh my goodness! Do you have any idea how it could've happened?"

"I only spoke briefly with the police. They, of course, asked all the questions. But it sounds like foul play was involved. They think he could have been drugged or poisoned based on how his body was found."

She tapped a pensive finger over her lips. "Doesn't it seem strange that he had an outburst at the meeting and turned up dead outside just hours later?"

"Last night's meeting was tense, but I never could have imagined it could end in"—even I struggled to utter the last word of my sentence—"murder." Saying the word somehow made the situation more real.

Ava shook her head. "Based on what we saw, I wouldn't be surprised if that guy had an enemy who'd want him dead."

Sensing Ava's discomfort and observing the random mix of ingredients spread out in front of her on the bar, I inquired about what she was concocting, in an effort to change the subject to something much less grim.

"I had an idea for our summer cocktail menu, and I wanted to try it out right away."

I joined her behind the bar, eager to learn more about her

idea. With our summer menu launching a few weeks later—and falling behind on developing a unique menu for the impending season—I was grateful for Ava's initiative. Working on our new cocktails was a welcome distraction from the recent tragedy. "I'm intrigued. Tell me more."

"It's a twist on a margarita, featuring guava front and center. It's pretty simple. I poured some tequila, triple sec, guava nectar, and a splash of coconut milk over ice in the shaker, and voila!"

She scooped some ice from the ice machine behind the bar into a fish-shaped glass, picked up the shaker from the bar, and poured the pink mixture, slightly opaque from the hint of coconut milk, over the ice. She garnished the drink with a tiny umbrella and a round, thin slice of lime. "If we can, I'd like to order fresh guava to take this drink to the next level."

"We can swing that for sure. This drink is beautiful. Do you have any ideas for a title?"

"I thought about calling it 'Shall I Compare Thee to a Summer's Day?'" She continued talking before I could react. "It's super long, but this drink tastes like a summer day in a glass."

"Is that from eighteen or twenty-eight?" Thanks to my full-blown Shakespeare phase in high school, I knew her drink title borrowed from one of his sonnets. I'd read many of his plays, sonnets, and poems and attended any production of his plays that I could. I'd even enrolled at a local university to become an English teacher myself, but I dropped out after one semester, realizing I preferred working full time and reading for enjoyment rather than for assignments. "I think it's 'Sonnet 18,' but I'm a bit rusty."

Ava shrugged. "So, what do you think?"

I loved the name idea. "A bunch of our names are a bit long, but customers always get a good laugh from our cocktail titles when they're ordering. And they love those literary references. Let's use it!"

"By the way, when I grabbed some ingredients from the supply closet, I noticed we were running low on DCDC vodka," Ava informed me. We featured Delaware Crossing Distilling Company liquors in a few of our most popular cocktails, always happy to shine a light on a fellow local business. "I placed an order with Logan, and he'll be delivering some bottles at some point later today."

"Sounds like a plan. Thanks for keeping an eye on our inventory."

I joined in on Ava's mixology fun by working on a summery coffee cocktail. I experimented with store-bought cold brew, but I planned to either brew my own in-house or partner with a local coffee shop. I loved the idea of collaborating with other businesses in town, not only to gain exposure for Subplot, but also to promote other local shop owners. I had no clue what I might create, but with coffee as my inspiration, I at least had a spark.

As we crafted our new drink ideas, a knock pounded on the downstairs door.

Oh, no. Ava and I froze and immediately locked eyes. We put our bar tools down.

I hoped this wasn't a bad omen.

I strode around the bar, taking my time to answer the door as if the person on the other side might go away if it took too long to answer.

Another knock thudded on the heavy metal door, echoing through the empty lounge. I froze in my tracks before proceeding. Was it the police?

I pushed the door's crash bar with a sweaty hand. Chills ran down my spine as a tall—at least six-foot two—frame appeared in front of me. After allowing my disorientation to wear off, I recognized my best friend Nate's prematurely bald head and wardrobe that might as well be sponsored by Carhartt. He wore a loose black T-shirt with a pocket over the left side of his chest, khaki cargo pants, and brown work boots.

I placed a hand over my chest and breathed quick, labored breaths. "Oh, it's just you."

"*Just* me? I guess I'm *only* your best friend, huh?" He stroked his thick, well-groomed strawberry blond beard. Growing up, Nate had bright blond hair, so when he first started to grow reddish facial hair during freshman year, it took everyone at our high school by surprise.

"What are you doing here?" I asked.

He rattled the toolbox hanging from his hand. "I had an opening in my day, so I figured I'd make some more headway on your office. Plus, it seems like we have a lot to discuss." He stepped to the side, giving me a clearer view of the alley. Though yellow caution tape secured the area by the dumpster where I'd found Brent's body, our door was still accessible.

In addition to being one of the greatest people I'd ever met, Nate was a talented handyman. Since renovations in Subplot's lounge, bathrooms, and kitchen had been a mad dash, finishing up the office had taken a backseat. For weeks, I'd been working under a lightbulb with no fixture around it.

"I take it you've heard about what happened?" My eyes drifted from Nate to the crime scene.

"One of my clients filled me in this morning." Nate was a jack of all trades and a go-to handyman for many businesses, landlords, and homeowners in town. He had his fingers on the pulse of all things Hope Mills, whether a new business was opening or closing, a special local event was taking place, or a rare scandal was happening. "At first, I didn't believe him, but then I checked the news."

I pressed both hands to the back of my head. "This is going to be terrible for business."

"Tell me everything." He stepped inside, allowing the door to close on its own behind him, and followed me to the bar.

After he placed his toolbox on the ground and slunk onto a stool, Ava and I summarized the events from the evening before.

Ava chimed in as I told the story. "That guy Brett—"

"Brent," I corrected.

"Whatever his name was. He was way out of line. I couldn't believe the way he spoke to everyone."

I shook my head in disgust as I recalled his disrespect.

"And the woman who stood up to him—Kristin." Ava's hands were animated as she recounted the prior night's events while sharing her perspective. "Everything she said was spot-on, but her approach was terrible. And then for Brent to turn up dead later in the night? It makes ya wonder what *actually* transpired."

I closed my eyes tightly and tried to erase the images from the night before from my mind. The discovery I'd made next to the dumpster haunted me.

"About that ..." Something about Nate's presence made me feel comfortable about sharing more. "When I took out the trash last night, I discovered Brent's body."

Nate and Ava's eyes appeared to be glued on as they bulged with disbelief.

"Reece, I'm so sorry. I didn't realize you found ..." Ava reached to place a concerned hand on my shoulder.

"No, it's okay." I swatted at the air as if I didn't care. "It was shocking, to say the least."

The two of them each cocked their heads in a way that said *Tell us more.*

"They're treating his death like a homicide." I explained

how Brent's body had been found, including the empty snifter glass beside him and the wallet missing from his person, although we'd seen him wave it around the night before. "There's no way we could have been responsible, but I'm worried it makes us look suspicious. Even if it doesn't come down to that, I'm concerned it will tarnish Subplot's reputation."

"We served him one small tasting glass of bourbon," Ava said. "If he was poisoned somehow, it couldn't have been done by either of us."

"And besides, who knows what he got into after he left the meeting," Nate added.

I scratched at my temple. "Yeah, I guess you're right." My dry mouth made it hard to speak and swallow. "I swear I never even knew he existed until yesterday. He treated everyone terribly at the meeting—from how he disrespected Will to belittling Logan and DCDC. It almost makes me wonder if there was some sort of history between them we don't know about."

Ava planted a fist on one hip. "I'm not gonna lie—I think Kristin knows something we don't. You heard the way she talked about Brent before he even arrived. And the way she spoke to him after he did? I'm not saying she killed him, but I have a feeling she at least knows something."

Nate's eyes followed Ava and me as we each spoke, clearly engrossed in our speculation.

I drummed my fingertips on the bar before looking back up at Ava. "I agree. It'd be a stretch to suspect she'd kill him solely based on his behavior last night, but who knows if she had a deeper motive. She clearly hated Brent, and it seems like it cut deeper than being annoyed by how he acted at whiskey club meetings."

Ava gasped and shifted her weight from one foot to another, placing her opposite hand on her other hip. "You know what? I just remembered. I see her all the time at Riverside Roastery. I *knew* she looked familiar yesterday. She must work remotely because she's there fairly often with her laptop in the corner."

"Hmm ..." I stroked the scruff on my cheek.. "Really?"

"I go to Riverside Roastery every day, and I'd say she's there three out of five weekdays, at least." Ava crossed her arms confidently. "She wasn't there this morning, but maybe she's there this afternoon. If not, you shouldn't have a hard time finding her there another day."

"If she had something to do with Brent's death, don't you think she'd try to lay low?"

Ava tapped a finger over her lips. "Not necessarily. If anything, I'd think she'd want to blend in and carry on as if everything's normal."

I lowered my left hand and checked my watch. Six minutes after three. I had almost two full hours before we had to prep the lounge for our Thursday evening service, which started another hour later at six. "I *do* have plenty of time to go for a quick coffee run," I said, making no mention of Kristin. "I *am* dragging a bit, so the caffeine would be a nice boost. Plus, since I'm working on a cold brew cocktail, I had an idea to partner with a local coffee shop on it. Maybe this is the perfect opportunity to try and meet the owner of Riverside Roastery and ask about collaborating. Do either of you want anything?"

Ava pointed at a plastic cup on the counter behind her, sweaty with condensation. "I've got my caffeine fix right over here. But I need some fresh air, so I might follow you out."

"I cut off my caffeine consumption after two, so I'll have to pass," Nate answered. "I should head back and take care of a few of these tasks in the office so I can be out of your way well before you open this evening. If you're both leaving, I'll be one thousand percent sure to lock up, especially considering the circumstances." I could always count on Nate.

Ava drew her eyebrows together and stared straight into my eyes. "And if you end up going to the Roastery, please be safe. If Kristin's up to no good, I don't want you getting hurt."

"Don't do anything stupid," Nate added.

I waved my hand dismissively. "I'll be fine. And if I can manage to bump into her, I'll make it seem like a total coincidence. The Roastery is usually busy, and we'll be in a public space."

"Alright—be careful. And be mindful of what you say. Who knows how she'll respond, and her voice can carry through a space." Ava chuckled at her own joke.

I smiled and shook my head at her wit. "Good point."

I had no clue what I might say or what I should ask Kristin —or if I'd even be brave enough to address the elephant in the room. However, I'd have to face my fear if I hoped to mitigate damage to Subplot's reputation—or better yet, discover who might have been responsible for Brent's death.

SIX

Riverside Roastery was aptly named for its proximity to the banks of the Delaware River. The coffee shop's rear exit led out to the Promenade, a cement-paved walking path parallel to the river which led to the local theater, Washington Playhouse, and the Aquetong Creek Dam waterfall.

A tinge of sadness crept up my throat as memories of my proposal to Chloe flooded back. Over a year and a half before, I'd popped the question to Chloe along the Promenade beside the Playhouse after watching a performance of her favorite play, *The Glass Menagerie*.

Though we both grew up and went to school in Hope Mills, I was two years ahead of her. We hadn't interacted until I was twenty-one, working my first bartending job at the upscale restaurant in The Flora House, a luxury hotel and banquet venue on the outskirts of town, where she was waitressing. We became fast friends, and we didn't officially start dating for another two years, when we each took on new roles in our hometown's thriving food and beverage industry. We dated for nearly seven years before I proposed near where I walked today.

The Delaware River shimmered under the cloudless sky, and

the lush trees from the other side of the river in New Jersey reflected on the placid water.

As I approached the coffee shop, I admired its idyllic façade along the Promenade, framed by four wooden posts which extended several feet beyond the building's exterior. Edison bulb string lights zigzagged between the posts and the building, though it was too early for them to be lit. Three small metal tables with matching folding chairs sat under the suspended strings of lights, and pink-and-yellow striped umbrellas in the center of each table shielded patrons from the sun.

The toasty scent of freshly roasted coffee beans filled my nostrils as I entered Riverside Roastery. The coffee shop hummed with light chatter, soft jazz music, and the white noise-like *shush* of milk steaming at an espresso machine.

In addition to admiring the atmosphere and ambiance in the Roastery—the exposed brick walls, French artwork, and floor-to-ceiling windows facing the vibrant blue, gentle river— I surveyed the café for Kristin.

Unfortunately, I didn't see her anywhere. I tightened my lips and sharply inhaled a shallow breath through my nostrils, feeling discouraged.

Even if I couldn't bump into her there, at least I could inquire about partnering with the Roastery on my cold brew cocktail and enjoy a relaxing moment in a day shrouded in darkness. In addition to discovering Brent's body, seeing Cam as a result kicked up a storm cloud of emotions I'd been repressing.

And on top of the alley behind Subplot being declared a crime scene, I hoped gossip around town surrounding Brent's tragic death wouldn't deter customers from visiting the lounge.

The coffee bar was in the center of the café, situated between the front entrance which led to Main Street and the back entrance I'd used on the Promenade side. When it was my turn in line, I ordered a medium iced Americano—unsweetened and with a small splash of almond milk. "Also, while I'm here, is your owner around? I opened the new cocktail lounge in town, and we'd love to collaborate on a coffee-inspired cocktail."

The barista extended her hand toward me. "That'd be me! I'm Tiana."

"Oh wow, it's so wonderful to meet you! I had no idea you owned the Roastery. I love your shop." I shook her hand.

"I'll get you one of my cards so we can chat more about it, but what did you have in mind?"

"I'm working on a summery cold brew and coconut rum cocktail. I thought about making my own cold brew in-house, but I also had an idea to collaborate. It might be a great way for us to cross-promote. If there's a way I could purchase the cold brew from you, I'd love to feature you on our menu, and maybe you could advertise the cocktail to your customers as well."

Her face lit up. "I absolutely love that idea. If there's anything I can do to lift up another local business, I'm in." She hunched down and searched under the counter. She handed me a business card and asked me to send her an email so we could work through the details. "And I'll have your iced Americano coming right up."

As Tiana prepared my order, the bathroom door to the left of the espresso bar opened, and to my surprise, Kristin walked out.

I felt my eyes widen as if they might bulge out of their sockets. My rush of excitement was quickly followed by a wave of regret. Trying to chase her down for answers felt like a risky move. Furthermore, I had no clue how to kickstart a conversation, especially considering the sensitivity of the topic.

As she marched from the bathroom to the shop's seating area, she recognized me and rushed in my direction.

"Can you believe it?" she asked with unblinking green eyes

and flared nostrils as she tugged at the soft sleeve of my long-sleeved Henley shirt.

I looked at her dumbfounded, unsure of what to say.

"You remember me, right?" Her piercing voice reverberated on the tall brick walls around us.

How could I forget?

I gave her a long blink and bobbed my head. "Of course I do. Kristin, right? From last night."

"Reece," Tiana called my name from behind the counter. "Here's your Americano."

I picked up my beverage from the espresso bar and thanked her.

Kristin lingered behind me even though my attention had clearly wandered to my beverage. "I'm sure you've heard about … you know … the body? In the alley behind your bar?" she whispered.

I allowed my eyes to drift down to the drink in my hand. "Sadly, I have. Isn't it tragic?"

She placed a hand over her chest. "I can't believe such a thing would happen. And in Hope Mills of all places? Stuff like that doesn't happen here." Perhaps realizing there were other people within earshot, she pointed at a table in the corner of the café with an open laptop and a coffee mug on top of it, away from the other patrons. "Follow me."

"Uh … sure …" I hoped Kristin read me as hesitant. I wanted to learn more about Brent while also holding my cards close to my chest.

If I could uncover why he was so outwardly negative toward so many people at the meeting, I hoped I might learn why someone might've wanted him dead. Anything I could uncover was a step toward proving that Subplot had nothing to do with his demise. If I hoped to run a profitable business and pay off the business loans looming over my head, I had to keep our reputation squeaky clean.

Her shoulder-length curly blonde hair bounced in front of me as I followed her to the table. As we set down our coffees and took a seat, I noticed a brown leather bracelet on her wrist with a tiny silver raccoon charm dangling from it.

"I love your bracelet." I slid the phone out of my pocket, illuminated the screen, and showed it to her. The wallpaper on my phone lock screen was a picture of a baby raccoon grasping for a flower. "I'm a big raccoon fan myself." I chuckled. My social media algorithms fed me endless cute raccoon memes and videos.

She pinched the charm between two fingers and lifted her arm so I could get a closer glimpse. "Don't you just love their little fingers? They're the cutest little creatures."

I was grateful that my genuine compliment and mention of raccoons cracked her abrasive demeanor.

I pointed at her laptop. "What do you do for work?"

"Freelance content writer by day, and borough councilwoman by night."

I raised my eyebrows. "That's awesome. I'm sorry I didn't make the connection that you were on the council." I would've expected one of our town's representatives to have acted with more dignity than she'd shown the night before.

"You must not have voted for me, then." She chuckled. "I'm kidding. So anyways ... last night ..."

"Yeah. The meeting was ... interesting."

She puffed her cheeks up with a nervous breath as her intense emerald eyes threatened to stare through my soul. "Tell me about it." She spoke through clenched teeth. "This is bad. Really, really bad. They're treating Brent's death as a murder."

"How do you know that?" I asked.

She lifted a hand to her forehead and rubbed one of her

temples. "Well, I guess word got out to the police that I *allegedly*"—she made an exaggerated wink—"made some unfortunate comments about Brent before he was found ... ya know." She closed her eyes and stuck out her tongue.

Wow. She was making light of the murder? I hoped she didn't presume I filled the police in on those comments.

"So, I guess I'm one of their suspects." She rolled her eyes. "Whatever. Let them look into me. I have nothing to hide."

I dipped my chin down slowly and pressed my lips together. "I'll admit he seemed"—I searched for a diplomatic word that would get my point across—"difficult at the tasting, but I still can't imagine what would drive someone to take his life."

She reached for her mug to take a sip, but realizing it was empty, she set it down on the table and sighed. "Well, as you can imagine, Brent was good at making enemies."

"What do you mean?"

Kristin pushed her laptop screen down so she'd have room to lean toward me, hunching over as if to make herself small. "I'm as shocked about his murder as anyone, but I wouldn't be surprised if someone had what they'd consider to be legitimate reason to ..." She sat back in her chair. "Well, you know."

"Brent said he was from Kentucky. And Will said he was a new Lifted Spirits member. Does that mean he just moved to Hope Mills?"

Kristin nodded.

"If he's new to town, would he have had the time to make enemies? Do you know what brought him here?"

She sighed. "Work, I guess."

"Do you know what he does?" I asked.

She avoided eye contact. "I have no idea." I couldn't tell if she knew more than she let on, but I had a feeling she wasn't sharing everything she knew.

I filed my questions about Brent away in the back of my mind, intent on learning more.

If Kristin wasn't willing to share more about him and why he was so good at making enemies, I wondered why she went out of her way to chat with me.

"So why did you have such a big problem with Brent, then?"

She scoffed. "Wasn't it obvious? He was obnoxious, and I couldn't just let him get away with it. You saw how he treated Will and Logan during the meeting. Heck, he even called your lounge musty. And you didn't even see how he acted at D'Amico's before the Lifted Spirits meeting."

"What did he do?"

"Oh, the usual." She grunted. "He was acting belligerent. Before Theo and I came down to Subplot for Lifted Spirits, we ate dinner at D'Amico's. Brent was also in the restaurant before the meeting, and he was slurping down drinks and starting to get messy."

"Was he alone? Or was he with someone?" I asked.

"He was alone. Sitting by himself at the bar. I think they might have overserved him. He ended up getting into an argument with that prissy lady who is always walking around from table to table."

"Heidi?"

"I don't know her name, but she's always dressed up and has perfect brunette hair. She acts like she owns the place."

I couldn't stop the smirk on my face. "If we're thinking of the same person, she *does* own the place."

Kristin shrugged. "Well, in any case, their interaction escalated, and he stormed out of the restaurant. I'm assuming he didn't pay, but I'm not sure."

"He would've had to walk back into the building to come down to Subplot for the meeting later. I wonder if someone from D'Amico's saw him enter the vestibule and was able to flag him down," I reasoned as Tiana blended a frozen drink behind the espresso counter, filling the echoey coffee shop with noise.

"Who knows? But that's why I felt so fired up and acted how I did. I couldn't believe how he'd behaved at dinner, and I hoped with all my might he wouldn't show up to our meeting because I was sure he'd ruin it. And I know I said some things about Brent I regret, but I wanted you to understand where it came from."

Though I winced at the thought of having a conversation with Heidi, I wanted to learn more about her negative encounter with Brent. Whether I wanted to discuss his murder or not, it seemed inevitable she'd bring it up on her own—and likely find a way to blame me.

Ever since I signed the lease for the basement space which became Subplot, Heidi warned me not to invite any *unsavory* behavior into her space. She loved to use that word, and she used it often. It was difficult to avoid my upstairs neighbor on a normal day, so how hard would it be to find her at a time when I *wanted* to speak with her?

I peeked at my watch, and though I was still good on time, I used it as my excuse to leave. "I appreciate you talking with me about all of this, but I've got to head out to prep my lounge for this evening."

"Alright, be safe out there," Kristin said as I wrapped up our conversation and told her to do the same.

If I intended to get to the bottom of Brent's murder, I needed to learn more about who he was and why someone might have wanted him dead. But how?

SEVEN

I picked up my plastic cup, which was sweating with condensation and still nearly full. Feeling the tension surrounding Brent's death, I decided to take the long way back to Subplot, hoping the extra steps and fresh air might bring me some peace.

I meandered along the Promenade and sipped on my bold Americano while listening to the water flowing down the Delaware and chickadees singing from nearby trees. Light, savory grill smoke lingered on the air as I strolled past restaurants near the waterfront. Though the sunlight warmed my skin, the cool breeze sent an occasional shiver down my spine.

A fearful heat arose on the back of my neck after I slipped my phone out of my pocket and read one of the text notifications awaiting me. It was from Chloe.

> Hey Reece, Cam filled me in on what happened
> at the lounge yesterday. Are you okay?

After breaking off our engagement, Chloe and I had several weeks of distance and no contact, but in the few weeks leading up to the murder, we kept finding our way back to one another.

Between random encounters around Hope Mills to exchanging each other's belongings we discovered after the breakup, we were still untangling our lives.

Though I was still hesitant to face Chloe for another deep conversation, I appreciated her for checking in on me. Considering how upset her family had been about the breakup—and understandably so—I admired her for wanting to remain peaceful.

Even when we were dating, the line between friendship and romance was indistinguishable, which felt like an ideal state. Didn't everyone want to be in love with their best friend? Whether we were traveling to a music festival, on a hiking trip, or reading on the couch in our shared apartment on a chill Monday night, she was my safe place.

Despite our love, I couldn't shake the feeling something was missing from our relationship. I felt it when a handsome customer sat at the bar where I was working. I felt it when I saw two men holding hands while walking along the Towpath. I felt it when she and I went to the Philly Pride March to show our allyship, yet I felt like I was hiding a light inside of me that desperately wished to shine. As our wedding date drew closer, the feeling that I was being dishonest with Chloe—and with myself—grew more and more unbearable. And once we approached the six month mark in our countdown, I knew I had to make a big decision.

I told Chloe I was gay when I broke off our engagement. I assured her I never cheated or did anything to betray her trust. I wanted to be completely honest with her, and I couldn't be if I wasn't living in my own truth.

Although she was devastated, she handled my coming out with grace, promising me her support and that she wouldn't out me. Besides her, only Nate knew. I hadn't even told Ava, and I spent more of my waking hours with her than anyone.

Hi babe, I typed before erasing the term of endearment. It was such a hard habit to break, especially considering how much love I still felt for her.

> Hi Chlo, I'm doing alright. Just shaken up. I know I'll be okay. Thanks for checking on me.

I didn't want to worry Chloe with details, though her brother might've already given her info that didn't paint me in the best light. Perhaps he'd told her I found the body or that I'd interacted with the disgruntled victim hours before he died.

> I know Cam and team are working hard on the case, so I'm sure it will all work itself out

At the end of the Promenade, I turned onto the sidewalk along Main Street, which served as the main drag through Hope Mills, as well as being the home of D'Amico's and Subplot.

My phone buzzed in the front pocket of my tan chinos.

> Can we meet up to chat soon? There's something I need to share with you.

> As long as you don't tell Cam

With Cam and Detective Sharp investigating Brent's murder, I didn't want to be seen meeting up with Chloe, especially if they saw me as a person of interest.

> I won't – I promise

One thing about Chloe: if she said something, she meant it. When she made a promise, she kept it. And I trusted this still applied to me, even if I'd turned her world upside-down not long before the supposed-to-be happiest day of her life.

Did she want to talk about our relationship? Or did she have details about the murder to share?

> Where should we meet?

I ambled down Main Street, venturing up and down side streets to waste time. I passed May's Flowers floral store, an art gallery, a vintage clothing store, a newly opened bookstore, a vacant storefront with a sign that read CRESTMORE ENTERPRISES in the window, Jackie and Jill's bakery, a bunch of bars and restaurants, and pocket parks where people often stopped to socialize.

A-ha! The perfect place to meet up.

I went back to my text conversation with Chloe and sent another message.

> Could we meet up sometime at the pocket park near the corner of Main Street and Ridge Ave?

The pocket parks were relatively secluded recreation areas scattered throughout town, mostly between businesses. Most of them consisted of a bench or two, a couple of shrubs or a flowerbed maintained by the local beautification committee, and perhaps a sculpture or historic Revolutionary War monument. If Cam caught the two of us together, we could easily play it off by saying we ran into each other walking around town.

My phone buzzed in my pocket seconds after I slid it back in.

> Sounds good to me. When works for you?

> Are you around this weekend?

> Yeah, I'm pretty open Saturday and Sunday during the day. Let me know. I can be flexible

> Sounds good to me. I'll be in touch

Though I could've confirmed plans during our text conversation, I was hesitant. Had I not broken up with her, Saturday would have been our wedding day. I wasn't sure what emotions it might drum up, and I didn't know if I was ready to see her that day.

I watched three dots blink across the bottom of the screen as I awaited her next message.

> I still love you.

I clenched my eyes shut, but all I could see were the tears flowing down her face, her skin flushing, and the way she crumpled over on the day I broke her heart. I'd pulled out a critical Jenga block in the tower we'd built, causing it to collapse. And within an instant, she was left to pick up the pieces.

Though the end of our relationship was complicated—and this murky aftermath phase made matters even more difficult and complex—I knew she was telling the truth. Chloe didn't say anything she didn't mean.

> I love you too, Chlo.

And I meant it, too.

EIGHT

As the time approached 4:30, my afternoon relaxation reached its end. At five, Ava and I would enter full-swing preparation mode to open the cocktail lounge for our Thursday night service.

I wandered down Ferry Street and back to Main Street, where I made my way to D'Amico's and Subplot.

As I stepped through our shared foyer, I first spotted Heidi's petite frame wearing a flowy white blouse from behind through the glass double doors. She was facing Cam and Detective Sharp, and it appeared they were interviewing her in the otherwise empty restaurant.

I hadn't noticed a police car in front of the restaurant or on any of the side streets as I was walking, so their presence caught me off guard.

Did she have cameras that might help the authorities solve the case? I hoped so, but I also couldn't stop my curious mind from thinking of other reasons they might be speaking to Heidi. Had Kristin tipped them off about her altercation with Brent the night before?

Wanting to avoid them, I pivoted toward Subplot's bookcase entrance. But before I could fumble the keys out of my pocket to unlock my door, Cam entered the vestibule and called my name.

I froze in my tracks and slowly turned toward him.

He removed his hands from his hips and walked toward me. Detective Sharp finished scribbling notes in her pocket note-book after speaking with Heidi and joined us in the vestibule.

"Mr. Parker," Detective Sharp, dressed in a brown pant suit, nodded firmly at me.

"Detective." I returned the nod. "How's everything going with ...?" My voice trailed off.

Cam and Detective Sharp glanced at one another, prompting the detective to respond with a shrug. "We can't share any details. It's coming along. We're making progress and interviewing some leads."

"Leads?" I responded, hoping the detective might say something more.

Detective Sharp squinted and leaned toward me. "We've uncovered some evidence which has further confirmed our suspicion that foul play was involved."

I couldn't help but glance at Heidi, who stood with hands on her hips and an angry smirk on her face, over the detective's shoulder.

"If there's anything else I can do to help, I'm happy to," I offered.

Why would you say that, Reece? Though I knew any additional questions I answered might expose me to increased speculation, I truly wanted to help in any way I could.

After the police departed, I had no choice but to face Heidi, who was standing on the other side of her glass doors, arms crossed and hips leaning against the podium at the front of D'Amico's, waiting to chat.

I would've preferred a follow-up questioning by the police

over having to deal with Heidi's scrutiny, but avoiding her would get me nowhere.

"So, you're brown-nosing with the police, I see." Heidi tapped her foot on the ceramic tile floor as I stepped into the restaurant.

I resisted an urge to grunt, instead playing it off as a cough. "I'm cooperating with them. There's a killer on the loose somewhere, and I want our town to be safe."

Heidi pressed her fingertips into one temple. "What a headache."

"Tell me about it." Hopefully, the heat on my face didn't manifest as blushed cheeks or blotchy red patches crawling up my neck.

Heidi stood up straight. "How could you possibly relate? You invited this *unsavory* behavior into *my* building, and I'm stuck cleaning up *your* mess. I'll have you know that I've already informed Mr. Percy about this, and he's not happy."

Stan Percy, our landlord, had owned our shared building for forty years. For over half that time, D'Amico's Italian restaurant had been the sole tenant, but in the last year he had the property rezoned to accommodate a second tenant and earn additional income, and Heidi wasn't happy about it one bit. She jumped at any opportunity to complain about my clientele, the volume of the DJ we hired on Friday nights despite the soundproofing Nate installed, and the influx of questions her staff received about my lounge since we shared a common breezeway. However, she never acknowledged how much busier her restaurant had become since Subplot opened.

"D'Amico's has been an institution of downtown Hope Mills for decades, and I've been a reliable tenant the entire time. Mr. Percy and I have a wonderful relationship, and he's very accommodating to me, so I'd tread carefully if I were you."

I furrowed my brow. "Heidi, please believe me—this whole

situation has been dropped in my lap just as much as it has been in yours. Plus, I discovered the victim's body in the alley by the dumpster, and I can't unsee it. I'm sure the police were just dropping by to see if you saw anything or had any camera footage, right?"

Heidi's tall wedges clomped as she took heavy strides toward a nearby table draped with a white tablecloth. She pulled out a gold-framed chair with pink-striped upholstery and slumped into it. She held her head in her hands. "Reece, you don't understand. The police officer and detective think *I* killed the guy."

"What!?" I feigned ignorance. "Why would they suspect you?" I took a seat across the table from her.

She spat out an exhausted breath, allowing her lips to vibrate as she forced it out. "It's that dumb woman's fault."

"Who?"

"The blonde one with the loud mouth. She's on our borough council. She ate here before going to the disgraceful meeting in *your* lounge that caused this mess."

"Kristin?"

She shrugged. "I don't know her name. She was here with some other guy from their club."

"Why would she blame you?"

"It had to have been her. She probably saw ..." She stopped herself from continuing. "Plus, she's a loudmouth. Have I mentioned that yet?" It seemed like she was attempting to change the subject.

"Yes, you have." I bit the inside corners of my mouth to fight back a smile. "What do you think she saw?"

She closed her eyes and shook her head before reestablishing eye contact. "The guy who ended up being ..." She paused, as if suffocated by her words.

"I know what you mean," I said, freeing her from saying the word *murdered* out loud.

"He gave me a lot of grief, arguing with me about paying for his food at the end of his meal and accusing me of charging him for things he didn't order." She threw up her hands beside her face. "He was fuming mad, yelling at our staff and interrupting other customers' meals. It was humiliating."

I raised my eyebrows. "Do you think he was drunk?" I wanted to dig into Kristin's assertion that Brent had gotten sloshed at D'Amico's, although I still had doubts.

Heidi let out a sharp scoff as if I'd slapped her. "If he was, it wasn't from any drinks he had here. We didn't serve him any alcohol."

Kristin had been pretty insistent that Heidi or someone from D'Amico's overserved Brent. If Heidi claimed they didn't serve him any alcohol, one of them had to be lying. And if there were lies, there had to be something worth hiding behind them.

I wasn't about to admit it to Heidi, but it made sense that Kristin's testimony sent the police to D'Amico's to look for clues. However, I had yet to discover if Kristin's recollection was accurate or if it was meant to be a distraction from a darker motive on her part.

"Well, regardless of whether you served Brent any alcohol, maybe the police heard about his tirade here and thought you might have more info to fill the gaps."

"Excuse you!" She raised her voice. "You know what they say about people who make assumptions."

I sighed and pinched the bridge of my nose with my thumb and index finger. "I'm not saying you did anything wrong, Heidi. I'm sure you handled the situation perfectly last night. But even if you did everything right, the victim still caused a scene in here, which—from an outsider's perspective—might make it look like you had a reason to commit the crime. But as I think we can both rationally say, being a difficult customer is hardly a reason to kill someone."

"If it were, I could have filled a cemetery in my career."

I winced. Maybe not the most appropriate thing to say, considering the circumstances.

"As long as you cooperate with the police and answer their questions honestly, you'll be just fine," I reassured her.

She harrumphed. "There's not much for me to tell them. I'm not usually one to brag about having a boring life, but I guess it serves me well."

If Heidi and Brent had been arguing, could she have slipped something into his drink before the Lifted Spirits meeting? I resisted the negative thought, not wanting to automatically assume the worst.

I scratched my beard. "The police need to speak to everyone who interacted with the victim in the hours leading up to their death. It doesn't necessarily mean they suspect you."

"Well, aren't you a walking and talking episode of *Law and Order*?" she snarked. "I sure hope you're right. I can guarantee I had nothing to do with this." She grabbed a cloth napkin from one of the table settings near us and dabbed her sweat-glistened forehead with it. "As for you ..." She pointed an accusatory finger in my direction. "You best keep your cocktail lounge under control. If you're overserving people down there, not only are you encouraging *unsavory* and reckless behavior in our peaceful town, but you're also inviting *and* unleashing them into *my* restaurant. If the slightest suspicious incident happens around here, the Hope Mills Police Department will be the first phone call I make."

I should hope they'd be your first call.

I nodded solemnly and pressed my palms together, trying my best to look sincere and hide my annoyance. "Heidi, you have my word. I'll do my absolute best. My lounge is all about the *craft* and *enjoyment* of cocktails, not about getting drunk. Are there customers who have a different idea? Sure. But the majority of them are interested in craft, not in going on a bender. I can promise you that."

Heidi glared at me. I think her warning was meant to make me feel responsible so she could turn blame away from herself. She could blame my lounge for attracting *unsavory* behavior all she wanted, but I still intended to find out if she'd contributed to Brent's misconduct.

"I guess I better head downstairs." I glimpsed at my watch. "I know you're about to open for dinner, and Ava and I need to finish our prep." I turned around, ready to head toward the vestibule.

"But wait!" Heidi urged, grabbing my forearm as I turned away. "Speaking of Ava ..." She lowered her voice to a hiss. "There's something else I need to share with you. It might be important."

I swiveled around to face her. "What is it?"

She exhaled deeply with her eyes closed. "Last night, when I locked our main door right before close in the foyer, I heard two voices outside on the street. They were distant, so I couldn't make out what they said, but it sounded like arguing. When I poked my head out the front door, I spotted Ava and the guy from the distillery walking away from the restaurant down Main Street."

If Heidi saw Ava with Logan, it must've been after I told Ava she was free to leave mid-way through the meeting the night before. They both had left the Lifted Spirits meeting at about the same time. What could they possibly have been arguing about?

I squinted. "Are you *positive* it was Ava and Logan?"

"Pretty sure." Heidi examined her fingernails as she spoke. "I saw a petite woman dressed in all black with long, straight black hair and a rugged looking guy with long blond hair and a backwards hat."

That was a description of Ava and Logan if I'd ever heard one.

Heidi finished inspecting her nails and tucked her hands into the back pockets of her black skinny jeans. "As you mentioned, I guess we better finish getting ready to open for the evening. But do what you will with that information."

NINE

"The Perks of Being a Wallflower drink sounds delicious," a woman who appeared to be in her late twenties dressed in an olive-green romper said. The drink was lovingly and eponymously named after the Stephen Chbosky novel. It was a twist on an Old Fashioned cocktail, incorporating lavender as its accent flavor and garnish rather than orange.

The man accompanying her, who I presumed to be her date, scanned the menu.

All of our menus were replicas of classic hardcover books, and each featured a different title on the spine. Because of this, each table had a unique stack of classic novels on it, making my cocktail lounge look like a book lover's paradise.

Our menu offered an equal number of *Fiction* cocktails, which contained alcohol, as well as *Non-Fiction* alcohol-free mocktails.

"I'll have ..." the man, clearly indecisive, hesitated. "Let's do the Huckleberry Gin." The cocktail was, of course, named after the Mark Twain novel.

"Ooh, great choice!" I commented. The cocktail was simple: gin shaken with fresh lemon juice and house-made huckleberry preserves. Then, we strained it over ice and a teaspoon with a small scoop of the preserves on it. "I'll get to work on those."

Since Subplot's grand opening several weeks before, we'd been consistently busy. In fact, we often couldn't accommodate everyone who wanted to stop into the lounge, so our maître d' Lainey helped us manage our wait list at her podium upstairs, as we did not take reservations.

Thursdays, although technically a weeknight, were the unofficial start to the weekend in Hope Mills. Many restaurants, including D'Amico's, offered Thursday night specials and events to draw locals and visitors out on the town, and they usually came out in droves.

Despite it being a Thursday, I'd expected a slower evening in the aftermath of the previous night's events and the news spreading around town. Surprisingly, the lounge was as busy as ever. Rather than question the reasons why, I instead maintained gratitude for the business and focused on serving our guests.

I jogged behind the bar to make cocktails for the couple I'd waited on as Dante, our server, carried a tray of four drinks away from the bar and over to another table.

Craft cocktails required a lot of work and attention to detail. Although Ava and I mostly stayed behind the bar to focus on perfecting drinks while Dante waited on customers, we still enjoyed interacting with patrons whenever we could, and it helped us stay in the know about what they enjoyed most. We usually waited on customers at the bar and at a few seating pods while Dante waited on everyone else and assisted with clearing tables, dishes, and cleaning up any spills that might happen.

I loved getting into a rhythm behind the bar. Shaking up a cocktail made me think of my dad, who taught me there was an art and science to crafting the perfect cocktail. One year when I was a teenager, he traveled to Italy to compete in the Martini Grand Prix, which is one of the most prestigious international cocktail competitions in the world. Although he didn't win, his desire to compete taught me from an early age there was much more to mixology than getting drunk.

Instead, it was about getting innovative with flavor. It was about having a shared experience with a community. In the same way it could bring loved ones together, it could also forge new friendships with strangers. And if abused, it could cause anger, arguments, division, and unruly behavior—even ruining relationships and lives. My menu offered both cocktails and mocktails so everyone could feel welcome to participate in the community mixology could foster.

My stomach turned as I thought about coming out to my parents. Though I knew they loved me, they—particularly my mom—were upset about my broken engagement. If they knew I was gay, would her pestering about grandchildren ever stop?

After I finished making the cocktails, I carried them out to the couple, who'd inched their chairs closer since I'd taken their order.

"One Huckleberry Gin and one Perks of Being a Wallflower." I set each glass on the table in front of them.

As I turned around to wait on a party Lainey had just seated, I almost collided with a man wearing a suit.

"Sorry, Reece—I guess I wasn't paying attention to where I was going," the familiar voice said, although I was too caught off-guard to recognize who it belonged to.

I took a step back and scanned the man from toe to head. It wasn't until I noticed his salt-and-pepper hair and lean frame that he registered in my brain as Will.

I opened my palm and clapped it together with his for a shake. "No worries at all. I was in such a flow and didn't see you coming."

"I'm headed to the bar."

I gestured toward a few open barstools. "Make yourself at home, and I'll swing by in a couple of minutes."

He gave me a firm pat on the back and headed to the bar.

I waited on the group of guys I'd been heading toward when I ran into Will, then built their cocktails behind the bar near where he was seated.

"I'm so relieved you're doing good business here tonight," Will said from his stool as I loaded ice into a shaker.

I answered in the softest tone possible, so as to not be over-heard. "I know. I was worried, but it doesn't seem like the bad news stopped anyone from coming out tonight."

After dropping the drinks off to the nearby group, I returned to take Will's order. He wanted a cocktail called A Rum of One's Own, named after Virginia Woolf's essay.

"You wouldn't have a moment to chat, would you?" He surveyed the lounge, perhaps to judge how busy we appeared. "I have something to tell you. It's related to last night."

We were slammed. Between taking orders and crafting drinks, I was in a constant state of movement. However, the promise of learning new information that might close the crime scene was hard to resist.

"Uh, sure. I can chat for a little bit. What's up?" I leaned over the bar.

He glanced around in all directions. Besides the couple seated at the far, opposite end of the bar—who were about to break into a make-out sesh by the looks of it—no one was around, and everyone was too engrossed in conversation to be able to make out a private discussion. Plus, the soft house music pulsing through the lounge made the conversations of anyone in our vicinity unintelligible.

Will sighed. "This afternoon, I left my office for lunch in town. I was walking to Sid's Sandwich Shop, and as I turned the corner to Main Street, I saw …" He stopped speaking and mouthed, *Ava*.

"Okay …"

"She sat alone on a bench and looked quite upset," he stared into his rum cocktail. "In fact, she was crying. Not a full-on sob, but tears streamed down her face, and she wiped them away with her wrists. I don't want to tell you what to do, but maybe you could check on her. See if she's okay, you know?"

Across the lounge, Ava was all smiles as she chatted with customers. If she'd been upset and crying earlier in the day, I surely hadn't seen it.

Will continued. "I, of course, recognized her from yesterday and thought she might've been upset about what happened after last night's meeting. I considered trying to comfort her, but her phone rang, so I kept my distance. I don't think she noticed me, so please don't mention I told you."

If what Will said was true, it broke my heart to know Ava might be carrying stress or guilt about what'd happened the night before.

I frowned. "Thanks for letting me know. I'll check on her later to make sure she's alright." I allowed my shoulders to relax and stared at the thick padded mat below my feet.

Though I planned to take Will's story seriously and follow-up with Ava, we'd discussed the murder earlier in the day, and the topic hadn't seemed to upset her. "I hope she isn't taking any responsibility for what happened. But trust me—I can understand how jarring it is to have been around someone who was killed hours later. It's been haunting me all day. I'm sure it's the same with you."

Will's lips pressed together. "Yeah …" His caramel eyes scanned the vicinity again. "But that's not what I'm getting at. When she answered her phone, she was flustered. I hate to admit to eavesdropping, but after everything that's gone down in the last twenty-four hours, I couldn't resist. So, I tucked in between two buildings and listened in."

"Did you hear anything?"

"I didn't make out every word, and I have no way of knowing what was being said on the other end of the line, but one thing she said for sure was, 'If they find out, my career is over.'"

I squinted at Will. "Are you *sure* she said that?"

"Positive. I thought you should know so you can keep an eye on her."

I felt a lump form in my throat. Was he implying that Ava might've had something to do with Brent's murder?

Will grunted, and his gaze drifted down the bar.

I spun my head in the same direction. Ava was back within earshot to my left.

As soon as she looked at us, I immediately averted eye contact as if I'd been caught committing a crime of my own.

"What?" She furrowed her brow before letting an uncomfortable laugh slip out.

I gulped. "Nothing."

She planted a fist on one hip. "Come on, you two. You guys aren't talking about me, are you?"

Will, arms crossed, panned his eyes toward her. "You caught us red-handed," he said before chuckling nonchalantly. "Just kidding. We were discussing what happened here last night, and I didn't want any customers to overhear. I'm still in shock."

Ava's deep brown eyes fell to the floor, and she didn't respond.

Rather than add to the conversation, I grabbed a towel from below the bar and flung it over my shoulder, ready to wipe down the area where the couple had just left.

I had my doubts about Will's observations, but I felt uneasy considering both he and Heidi claimed to witness suspicious behavior from Ava within the prior twenty-four hours.

Ava resumed preparing cocktails for Dante's tables. As I squeezed between her and the tight bar to catch up with each of the tables I'd neglected while talking to Will, I couldn't fight the whiff of suspicion I felt creeping in.

Did Ava know more than she let on? I hated it was even a possibility.

TEN

"I heard *he* found the guy," I overheard a customer, who was a bit tipsier than he realized, say from the seating pod nearest to me. I was mortified as the man with slicked-back gray hair pointed directly at me as I finished smoking an Old Fashioned cocktail with a blowtorch behind the bar.

"Yeah," one of the women accompanying him slurred. "I hope we're not being served by a literal murderer tonight."

The whole table laughed at her remark.

My stomach dropped as the weight of their theory sunk in. Did other people think I might have had something to do with Brent's death? They might not have known the facts of what had happened, but I realized that gossip would spread around our small town regardless. I didn't look up to acknowledge the customers. Instead, I stayed focused on slicing a strip of orange peel, twisting it into a spiral, and garnishing the Old Fashioned.

I sidestepped to wait on another couple Lainey had seated at the end of the bar as Ava continued to crank out cocktails for Dante.

As I prepared their drinks, the downstairs entrance squeaked open.

Oh no. What now?

Customers' heads throughout the lounge rotated toward the door, and a hush fell over the intimate lounge. The downstairs door was rarely ever used while the lounge was open, and considering what had happened there the night before, I could relate to the collective wariness.

Logan backed inside, propping the door with his body, and dragged a hand truck loaded with several boxes into the lounge. As he allowed the weighted door to close behind him, he noticed all eyes were on him. He pressed his lips together and gave the room a friendly wave. "Sorry." He grimaced and bowed his head.

As patrons resumed their conversations, Logan stopped at the bar. "Well, that was awkward. Sorry for the mid-shift delivery. It's been a busy day, and I heard you were running low on vodka."

"No worries," I reassured him. "Better than us running out."

Ava perked up as she delicately placed a sprig of rosemary into a drink she was finishing. "I can help you load those in the stock room," she told Logan without looking at him.

I thanked her, remembering our conversation from earlier in the day when she mentioned running low and placing an order. I pulled the lid off the cocktail shaker I was using and replaced it with a strainer as I prepared to pour the beverage into a glass.

After Logan pushed his hand truck to the stock room with Ava trailing behind him, my gaze shifted to Will, who sat patiently at the end of the bar with his credit card out. *Check, please,* he mouthed while scribbling a finger in the air.

I nodded and closed out his tab before delivering the cocktails I'd made and doing another lap around the lounge.

With his observation of Ava in mind, I remembered what Heidi had shared. Was it possible that Ava and Logan were continuing their argument in the stock room? Maybe I should've offered to help Logan unload.

Keeping up with the evening's busy pace, I made my way to a table in my area, in which Lainey had seated a group of young women who appeared to be celebrating a birthday.

"Don't worry. I checked all of their IDs," Lainey whispered on her way back upstairs.

A young woman in a white shirt with a light blue denim jacket seated next to the tiaraed birthday girl spoke up after I greeted the group. "Can we do eight shots of tequila, please? With limes and salt?"

I clenched my teeth together and drew in an audible, sympathetic breath. "Unfortunately, we don't offer shots here. Sorry." Subplot wasn't a typical bar. It was important to me that we focused on craft cocktails and delivering an exquisite and flavorful experience—not one that promoted a quick trip to intoxication.

The young woman sighed with disappointment. "Bummer."

"Not even for a birthday?" another young woman chimed in. "It's Sydney's twenty-first."

Before I could respond, another woman in the group interjected. "Could I have a Choose Your Own Adventure with a tequila base and a sweet and citrusy flavor?"

A nod to the classic interactive Choose Your Own Adventure children's books in which readers made decisions throughout the story to determine its ending, Subplot offered a menu option named after the series. Customers could name their spirit of choice and provide any other direction—whether they wanted a sweet, spicy, or spirit-forward beverage, or any other flavor request—and we'd create a custom cocktail on the fly. Not only did it keep us in an innovative mindset, but it also helped us discover new drinks which eventually became staples on our menu.

"Oooh, that sounds good. I'll have what she's having," the birthday girl added.

"I want one, too," another woman spoke up.

"Is that what we all want?" the original woman with the raspy voice and denim jacket—clearly the group's unofficial but understood leader—pointed among the circle of friends seated around a round coffee table. All the girls nodded. "So, I guess we'll have eight Choose Your Own Adventures."

I nodded with a satisfied frown. "That's easy enough to remember. Do you want me to make them all the same, or do you want me to make some variations based on those instructions?"

The group's coordinator looked around the circle at her friends with a shrug. "You can make them all the same so we can discuss it as we drink it."

A chuckle rumbled in my throat. "Alright, I'm going to get right to work on these. Are you all okay with mint?"

The young women nodded with enthusiastic approval.

I gave the group a thumbs-up. "Cool. Be right back."

I hustled behind the bar to begin crafting a tequila twist on a mojito inspired by the group's request. I grabbed a handful of mint leaves and smacked my hands together. Smacking the mint helped to extract the oils stored in the leaves, which helped to bring out the minty flavor in a drink. From there, I tore the leaves into smaller pieces and dropped them in a clean cocktail shaker. I added some fresh-squeezed lime juice, raw cane sugar, and tequila, then muddled the mixture before scooping in a heap of crushed ice. From there, I shook the mixture vigorously and poured it out over skinny glasses I'd already loaded with crushed ice and topped off each drink with a lime, freshly-smacked mint leaf, and an edible purple orchid. I had a feeling the flower—although added for the visual impact of its complementary bright color—would be a hit with the birthday group. The cocktail was photogenic, practically begging to be posted to social media.

After repeating the process a couple more times, I carefully loaded all eight cocktails onto a tray.

As I headed to the birthday group to deliver them, I spotted Ava stepping out of our one all-gender restroom. Based on the way she smoothed down her flowy black blouse and dipped her head, I sensed she was out of sorts. Perhaps Will and Heidi's observations were going to my head, but she appeared to be flustered.

The birthday girl's group collectively gasped as I unloaded the beverages on their table.

"Oh my goodness, these look like spring in a glass!" one girl commented.

"No one drink it yet!" the raspy-voiced ringleader of the group instructed. "We need to get a photo of these for social media!"

I was relieved the group was happy, especially after I'd declined serving them shots.

I rejoined Ava behind the bar as she built a beautiful pink grapefruit martini. Her black hair, usually perfectly smooth and silky, was frizzy and disheveled. She was typically energetic and confident, but her vibe felt drained and forlorn.

"Is everything alright, A?" I asked as I tapped out order updates in the point-of-sale and generated a receipt for a customer at the bar who was looking to close out.

Her response was delayed. "Yeah, I'm fine." Her sulking voice made me believe she was *not* fine.

Had something happened between her and Logan when he made his delivery?

I turned away from the bright LED touchscreen in front of me and gave Ava my full attention. "I know it's been intense around here lately. If you need *anything,* I have your back. I'm worried about you."

She poured more martini ingredients into a fresh shaker. "I found something in the restroom a little while ago." She firmly pressed a metal lid on top of the cocktail shaker and began to shake again before I had a chance to ask a follow-up question. She didn't shake the drink with the same vigor she usually put into it.

While I waited for a receipt to print, I kept my gaze fixed on her. "What did you find?" I asked as soon as she set the shaker down on the bar.

She trembled as she crouched down and reached for an item under the bar. "This."

It was a black leather wallet.

"That's not ..." I didn't finish my sentence.

Ava handed it to me.

I spun around to open it so no customers could see what I was doing.

I flipped it open and scanned the ID inside.

I gasped out loud as soon as I saw the face on a driver's license staring back at me.

ELEVEN

Brent Crestmore. The name was printed on his driver's license. I took note of his last name, which I hadn't known before.

Crestmore Enterprises. That was the company name printed on the business card peeping out of one of the wallet's interior pockets. Did he own Crestmore Enterprises? It seemed likely. What did his business do? I was determined to find out.

The business name was vaguely familiar, but I couldn't quite place where I remembered it from. I repeated it in my mind over and over as I wished for photographic memory. As tempted as I was to fish the phone out of my pocket and take a quick picture, my paranoia got the best of me. I didn't want any customers to see, nor did I want Ava to think I was up to no good.

1263 Wilson Drive, Hope Mills. I committed the address on his license to memory. Perhaps I could do a quick drive-by to see what I could learn about him.

There was no cash inside the wallet. Had whoever poisoned or drugged him robbed him as well?

That was all the information I could gather before I glanced over my shoulder at Ava, who was hovering behind me.

"What do we do?" Ava's breath was shallow.

"We definitely need to loop in the police."

"No!" she blurted out right away.

"This is an important piece of evidence," I whispered, hoping none of our customers were paying attention to us or wondering what was going on. "The police were looking for this when they showed up last night."

Detective Sharp hadn't found the wallet during her search, and I'd personally cleaned the restroom before the lounge opened for the evening, so it had to have appeared since we'd opened for the night.

"Oh my gosh." Ava covered her mouth with both hands. "And I moved it. I moved an important piece of evidence. I swear I thought someone just dropped it in the bathroom by mistake. I picked it up, saw who it belonged to, and I freaked out. I wasn't thinking. Do I put it back where I found it?"

I shook my head quickly. "Absolutely not. It has both of our fingerprints on it now. We need to tell the truth about what happened." I took a deep breath. If I wasn't a suspect already, would the police think I had something to do with this now? What if they thought Ava or I had it all along? If word got out about this, it wouldn't look good for Subplot. "And besides, if we put it back, there's a chance someone else might swoop in and take it. At least now we can be sure about getting it to the police."

"This is going to look so bad," Ava mumbled. "Are you sure we call the police? Can't we return it anonymously somehow?"

"No, we need to call them right away." I trusted that the police would do their job, and I wanted to make sure they had as much information as soon as possible to conduct their investigation.

"You guys?" Dante's voice called out from the side of the bar. "We're getting a bit backed up."

We each pivoted toward him, probably looking like children caught sneaking a cookie from the jar before dinner.

I held the wallet behind my back. "Sorry, we needed to huddle on something. We're ready to crank out some drinks."

I crouched down to stash the wallet on a shelf under the bar, hiding it behind a stash of pens and spools of receipt paper.

"Hey, team. We're going to have to close early tonight." I spoke into a tiny lapel mic clipped to my shirt, which was connected to an earpiece Ava, Lainey, Dante, and I each used to communicate. "Lainey, if you could please let any customers on our waitlist know and turn away anyone new who shows up, we'll finish serving everyone down here. We can finish any orders that have already been placed, but let's not take any new ones."

I hated having to close up shop early, especially considering how busy the evening was.

I couldn't stop my brain from calculating the revenue we stood to lose, the time it'd take to repay my loans, and—worst of all—the damage it might do to our reputation. I didn't want Subplot to appear flaky, but I also didn't want to waste any time informing the police of the discovery in our bathroom.

The rest of the shift was a whirlwind—serving the final round of drinks, closing out checks, and respectfully coaxing customers to leave without seeming like anything was wrong. I was also sensitive to Dante and Lainey. They hadn't been around during the Lifted Spirits meeting, and while they were aware of the nearby crime scene, I didn't want to burden them with details that didn't involve them.

As soon as the final customers left Subplot, I dismissed Dante and Lainey for the night.

"Are you sure?" Dante asked as he cleared a table. "But what about all of the dishes?"

Lainey rushed down the stairs. "And don't you need help wiping down tables and sweeping up? I'm happy to do it."

I crossed my arms. "Ava and I have it under control. You both can head out, and I'll still pay you your full hours." It was the least I could do.

Dante stepped toward me with a black plastic bin filled with empty glasses. "Is everything okay? Something feels a little off tonight."

I looked to Ava, whose hairline was glistening with small beads of sweat, and turned back to Dante. "Yeah. Everything's fine. With what happened outside yesterday, it's just been a lot. But we're a team, and we'll get through this. I think I just need some time. I should be all good to open back up tomorrow."

Once Lainey and Dante departed, I pulled the phone out of my back pocket and fidgeted with it in my hand.

Ava looked like a wreck. She'd been running her fingers through her hair, and she stared numbly into the dimly lit lounge.

"It's going to be okay." I dialed the numbers to Detective Sharp's direct line. "Here goes nothing."

"Why didn't you call the second you found this?" Detective Sharp flexed the wallet between her thumb and index finger.

I rubbed my palms together. "I called as soon as I could. We can explain."

Detective Sharp rested the wallet on the bar behind her, freeing up both hands to plant on her hips. "It's going to need to be a really good explanation. I'm very disappointed that you didn't call me right away. And the fact that this important piece of evidence was moved?"

Ava stepped beside me in the open area in front of the bar. "I treated it just like any other wallet I would've found." She twirled a tuft of her long, straight black hair around her finger. "I had to use the restroom in the middle of the shift. When I was in there, I saw the wallet on the ground. I picked it up and when I saw who it belonged to, I got scared. I didn't even know his wallet was missing. I was worried someone else might get ahold of it. I took it behind the bar to put it in a safe place, but now I realize I made a terrible mistake. It's my fault. I shouldn't have moved it. I'm sorry."

Although we typically kept lost items locked in our office, I backed Ava up. "I probably would've done the same thing."

"Alright, well that explains why it was moved." The detective pulled out the field notebook and pen from inside her cerulean blazer, ready to take notes.

"As soon as I realized it was Brent's wallet, we closed the lounge as soon as we could. We didn't want to create chaos and panic for our customers," I explained, unprompted.

"Do you realize that the person who left the wallet could have still been in the lounge? We could've figured out who brought it in here since it likely wasn't lying around for long."

The detective made a great point, and our err in judgment was clear.

She puffed out a heavy exhale. "Alright, can you please show me where exactly you found this?" she asked in a much calmer tone.

"Sure." Ava led the way to the single-occupant restroom, down a short hallway with doors that led to our small kitchen, my office, and our supply closet.

We stepped into the small restroom, which was relatively tight for the three of us.

Two of the bathroom's walls were exposed brick, and the other two were charcoal-painted drywall. A vanilla lavender candle warmer sat to the left of the sink on a floating countertop Nate had constructed. On a Bluetooth speaker in the restroom, we played audiobooks of classic novels and poetry, which always garnered compliments from customers.

Figuring that Stanley Kunitz reading his poem "The Layers" over the speaker wouldn't assist with the detective's questions, I turned it off, as much as I loved its reflection on grief and aging.

"It was right here." She pointed at a spot on the floor between the toilet and the sink.

Detective Sharp pulled a compact DSLR camera out of her blazer and photographed the restroom with Ava pointing to the spot where she found the wallet.

"It seemed like it was in an odd place if it just fell out of someone's pocket somehow," Ava commented. "It makes me wonder if it was left in here by mistake or if someone planted it purposely."

"One thing's for sure," the detective said. "Regardless of how it ended up in this restroom, it had to have been in the wrong hands. Let's go back to the main lounge."

We followed Detective Sharp back out to the lounge. On the way, I flipped on the overhead lights, and we all took a seat at one of the pods which consisted of four leather armchairs around an amoeba-shaped coffee table.

"Obviously, the two of you were here during the whiskey tasting. Was anyone else from last night also here today?"

Ava and I looked at one another as if to discern who should answer the question.

I cleared my throat. "Yes. Will, the president of the Lifted Spirits stopped by. And Logan from the DCDC distillery made a delivery tonight."

At the mention of Logan's name, Ava's chin fell to her chest.

"Did you have eyes on them the entire night?"

"I only saw Logan when he arrived for his delivery. I never

saw him again after he and Ava went back to the stock room to unload it. I saw Will for most of the time he was here. We were super busy, though, and I didn't see him leave. I was waiting on a group of young women celebrating a twenty-first birthday, and he must have left sometime around then."

"And you?" she asked Ava.

She jolted, almost like the question startled her. "I didn't interact with Will at all. Logan made a vodka delivery that I helped him unload in the back room."

"Did you have eyes on Logan the entire time he was here?"

Ava's eyes darted to me, as if I knew the answer the detective was looking for. "Um ..." she fumbled. "No. Sorry. He ... dropped off the vodka and left. I stayed in the supply closet for a couple of minutes after he left. I, uh ... needed a breather." She seemed as if she might have a panic attack, based on her shallow and irregular breaths as she fumbled through her response.

What had happened between Logan and Ava that made her feel like she needed to collect her composure? Though Ava hadn't initially seemed to be upset by Brent's murder, her increasing uneasiness gave merit to Will's observation of her earlier in the day. Also considering Heidi's mention of seeing Ava and Logan arguing the night before, I couldn't help but wonder what was going on between them. However, it was probably a stretch to wonder whether it had anything to do with Brent. I reprimanded myself for even allowing the thought to cross my mind.

Detective Sharp raised one eyebrow as she scribbled in her notebook. "And how about anyone from the restaurant upstairs. Have any of them been down here?"

That was an odd question. Was it possible she was curious about Heidi?

"I don't think so." I shrugged and looked to Ava, who shook

her head. "It's possible that someone from up there could've come down here, but I didn't see anyone. Then again, it was a pretty hectic evening."

"And have you had any conversations with your landlord recently?" Her questions were coming out of left field.

"We spoke a couple of weeks ago about some renovations that I was finishing up down here, but other than that, no." Luckily, Mr. Percy was completely supportive of all renovations I wanted to complete to bring the space to life. "But he wasn't around at all tonight if that's what you're wondering."

After answering a few more questions, Detective Sharp left Subplot, of course taking the found wallet with her. "I'll be in touch if I have any follow-up questions later. And please get ahold of me *immediately* if anything else pops up," she'd said on her way out.

I worried about whether she thought the wallet made me or Ava appear suspicious. If she was looking for a thread which connected Subplot to Brent's murder, it couldn't bode well for me or the success of my business.

Those fears aside, however, I couldn't stop my mind from wondering about her motivations to ask certain questions, particularly those relating to D'Amico's restaurant and Mr. Percy.

If I hoped to uncover the truth, protect Subplot's reputation, and return to business as usual, I needed to get to the bottom of Brent's murder.

I was going to have to take research into my own hands.

TWELVE

Aside from my passion for mixology, one of my favorite things about owning Subplot and working in the bar and restaurant industry was the flexibility it gave me while most people were working nine-to-fives.

While many Hope Mills residents were headed to work on a Friday morning, I was able to meet up at Riverside Roastery with my best friend Nate at nine a.m.

We often saw each other throughout the week or on my off days when time permitted, but we did our best to meet up for Friday morning coffee each week, sometimes followed by a hike on a nearby trail. Today, we were the only customers seated along the Promenade in the cool, breezy mid-fifties air. It was perfect sweatshirt weather.

"You can't catch a break, can you?" Nate commented more than asked, after I told him about Ava finding Brent's wallet the night before.

"It's been an intense week." As I traced my finger along the handle of my canary yellow mug, filled with a honey cardamom latte, I explained the combination of events—the pressures of running the lounge, the ongoing guilt I felt surrounding my broken engagement, my fears about coming out, and the murder investigation, including the wallet incident from the night before. "And did I mention who one of the officers on my case is?"

Nate rested his crimson mug, filled with steaming drip coffee on the composite wood table. His mouth hung wide open. "No." His tone suggested he already knew where I was headed.

"Yep." I slid my lower lip through my top teeth. "Cam."

Nate let out a small chuckle. "I mean, you have to admit it's kind of funny."

"What?" I squinted and craned my neck forward. "It's not funny at all. Awkward, is what it is."

Nate grunted. "You know what I mean. It's not *ha-ha* funny, but you have to admit—it seems like the world is messing with you."

"Well, the joke's on me." I shook my head. "We were almost like brothers before the breakup. It was the first time I'd talked to him since. And now he probably thinks I was involved somehow."

"Oh, stop it." Nate scrunched his eyebrows. "There's no way he thinks you had anything to do with it. Cam *knows* you. He knows you're not organized enough to pull something like that off, even if you wanted to."

"Hey!" I placed a hand over my chest, acknowledging Nate's friendly jab. "I was organized enough to get a small business loan and open this lounge in under six months. Isn't that worth anything to you?"

"True. Thankfully, you had a talented jack of all trades to help you pull it off. But pulling off a murder? You can't tell a lie. Remember when we planned to skip school and play video games back in high school while my parents were out of town? You completely chickened out on me."

I grinned at the memory. "I worried the office would call my parents if I didn't show up."

"Bro, you were supposed to call the office and impersonate your dad. You sound exactly like him!"

I rolled my eyes. "There's no way I could've gotten away with it. I would still be grounded today if I tried a stunt like that."

"Exactly. So how could Cam possibly think you killed someone? He knows you."

"After what happened between Chloe and me, I'm not sure he thinks so highly of me. He probably wouldn't be too sad to see me locked up."

Nate glowered at me, clearly annoyed with my logic. "Now *that's* not a statement I'm willing to co-sign for. Regardless of how he feels about your breakup, I'm sure there's no way he'd want you to be tied up in this."

I knew Cam led with integrity, and I should've trusted his professionalism. My doubts about him stemmed from my guilt surrounding the breakup.

"Does Cam even know the reason you ended it?"

I pursed my lips and shifted them to the left. "Honestly, I don't know. Chloe said she wouldn't tell anyone, and I trust her, but I wouldn't blame her if she did. I'm sure she's getting just as many questions and outside opinions—if not more—than I am. If my mom makes another comment about not getting grand-children ..."

He took a sip of coffee. "Any time I've talked to her since the breakup, she's been nothing but supportive." Throughout my relationship, Nate and Chloe formed a friendship of their own.

"Really?"

"One hundred percent. She's heartbroken, sure, but she completely understands and respects you." Nate slid his hand toward me and patted the table. "And you know what? I respect the heck out of you, too. I probably can't even fathom the amount of courage it takes to come out. But you didn't only do that—you also had to end a relationship and uproot someone else's life so you could live in your truth. And that's not easy."

Nate was the first person I came out to, and I was grateful for his immediate compassion and support. I told Chloe a couple of weeks later when I ended our relationship, but I hadn't told anyone else.

I always had an inkling I was gay, but I never explored the possibility. I lived my life the way I thought I was expected to.

Despite the expectations I felt to marry a woman and start a family, I truly fell in love with Chloe's soul, even if it felt like something was missing from our relationship—something that had nothing to do with her and everything to do with me.

"But ..." The words got tripped up in my throat. A pesky tear formed in my left eye. *Do not cry.* "Any way you slice it, I broke her heart. And I feel terrible about it. She spent every day planning our wedding and thinking about our happily ever after. Meanwhile, I spent my days contemplating whether I should end the engagement or hold onto my secret and live a lie forever." I couldn't stop the single tear from streaming down my cheek. Typically, I wasn't so emotional, but the events of the prior few days tested me.

"She truly loves you. She was about to spend the rest of her life with you. If anyone in this world would understand, it's her. She loves *you* for *who you are.* Have you talked with her about this since the breakup?"

I shook my head. "But she texted me yesterday. She wants to meet up to talk sometime. We haven't made concrete plans yet, but I offered to get together this weekend."

"I think you'd both feel better if you took her up on that. Especially since you've both had some distance, you can approach the conversation with some clarity."

"But this weekend, we would've been getting married."

"Maybe it'll give you both the closure you need."

I allowed my shoulders to slump. "You're right. And I owe it to her."

Nate smiled warmly. "Great."

He raised his mug toward me, and I followed suit. "Here's to pushing forward," he said as our mugs clinked together.

"It'll be a lot easier to press forward once they figure out who killed Brent—and why. A crime scene behind the lounge is a bad look. I heard some customers gossiping and making up theories last night. Plus, a missing piece of evidence showing up in Subplot? It makes me want to get to the bottom of this."

"As you should." A devilish smirk grew on Nate's face. "Based on everything you've told me, it sounds like you're already connected to people the police are talking to and asking questions about. The killer might have been in your lounge at the tasting. I don't think it'd hurt to take matters into your own hands—stealthily, of course."

If Nate sensed I was in a comfort zone, he loved to nudge me to step out of it. Just like trying to convince me to play hooky in high school.

"I should probably leave it to the police, although I feel like I have a few things I'd like to scope out."

Nate's eyes widened. "Like what?"

"After Ava found Brent's wallet, I memorized a few details about him. Brent Crestmore. Does that name sound at all familiar to you?"

He tapped his fingertips along the side of his mug. "It doesn't ring a bell."

"He had some business cards in his wallet for a company called Crestmore Enterprises. I'm assuming he either owned it or played a major role if it's a family business."

Nate scratched at his red beard. "Now that sounds familiar, but I can't put my finger on where I've seen it."

"And the address on his license was 1263 Wilson Drive. I've never even heard of that road, but it's somewhere in Hope Mills." Because of Nate's work as a handyman, he was constantly visiting different parts of town—particularly residential areas—that I never had a reason to visit, so I figured he might know more. "Do you know where that is?"

He nodded. "Wilson Drive is on the outskirts of town. There are a bunch of old farmhouses out that way." His impish grin returned. "Why? Do you think you'll do a little drive-by?"

I polished off the final sip of my latte. "I shouldn't. What if the police are there and they see me snooping around?"

"Let's take my truck. No one will suspect a thing. I'll just be"—he raised his hands to form air quotes—"*heading to my next job.*"

"Alright," I said, probably sounding reluctant, although I was internally bursting with excitement to see what I could learn. "Let's see what we can dig up."

We turned onto Wilson Drive, which was shaded by a canopy of lush green leaves. With my window opened a crack, I couldn't hear a peep besides birds chirping in the trees and the truck's tires rolling down the calm street.

"Wow, these homes are incredible," I commented as we coasted down the meandering street.

Most of the houses were large and set far back from the road with lots of space and wooded areas between them, creating plenty of privacy for their residents.

"That was 1259." Nate's speedometer was at twelve miles

per hour as we inched down Wilson Drive. "Here's 1261 coming up." The odd-numbered homes were on my side of the street.

We pulled up in front of a mailbox with TWELVE SIXTY-THREE WILSON DRIVE labeled on its side in gaudy cursive script. It stood in front of a long tree-lined driveway that turned into a mini cul de sac in front of a massive brick house.

"Brent must have been loaded," Nate commented. "Let's just call it what it is. This thing is a mansion."

"I'm so relieved there are no police here," I mumbled as I observed two cars parked in front of the house. "I wonder if anyone's in there."

"Want to find out?"

"No!" I urged through my teeth. "I have no clue if Brent was married or lived alone or what his situation was."

"If he could afford this home, he might even have had a live-in housekeeper. I think you'd need one to maintain a house and property of this size."

I sighed. "I'm thinking he made his money through Crestmore Enterprises, but without knowing what they did—"

Out of the corner of my eye, I noticed the silver compact car that had been parked in the driveway started to move forward. "Did you see that?"

The car picked up speed and zoomed down the long driveway.

I held my breath.

"See if you recognize who's inside," Nate said.

"I'll try." I slouched down in my seat as every muscle in my body tensed. I hoped the rearview mirror of Nate's truck might obstruct part of my face so that whoever was driving the car wouldn't see me.

As the car reached the end of the driveway with its driver's side window down, the car came to a rolling stop.

I shifted in my seat to catch a glimpse of the driver.

It was Kristin.

Though it was physically impossible from that distance, I swear I could make out the glowing emerald irises of her eyes. There was a deer-in-the-headlights expression on her face.

Unfortunately, I think she spotted me, too.

She squinted as if to confirm what she'd seen, turned her head away, and sped off down the otherwise silent street.

THIRTEEN

After my accidental run-in with Kristin outside of Brent's house, Nate drove us back to downtown Hope Mills. He'd told the owner of May's Flowers that he'd arrive at eleven to install new shelving. I still had several hours until I needed to get to Subplot to prepare for our Friday night service.

"Where do you want me to drop you?" Nate asked as we turned onto Main Street.

"Anywhere but on my head," I teased. "I'm going to swing by my landlord's office. The detective asked me if I'd spoken to him recently, and I need to figure out how he might be connected to the case."

Nate chuckled. "Oh wow, I didn't even have to persuade you this time. You're invested in this now, aren't you?"

He continued down Main Street and parked outside of May's Flowers. After getting out of his truck, we each clapped a hand together and pulled one another into a brief one-armed hug.

"Go get 'em," he said.

On my way to Mr. Percy's realty office, I strolled leisurely along Main Street, taking note of the movement in each of the storefronts and restaurants. The backs of customers seated at the bar of the Dublin Alehouse faced the window as I ambled past. I caught a whiff of fresh-baked bread as it wafted out of Jackie and Jill's Bakery next door.

And then I saw a sign in the window of an empty store-front that stopped me dead in my tracks. CRESTMORE ENTERPRISES.

A-ha! That's why the name rang a bell. I'd seen the sign the day before during my text exchange with Chloe. At that point, I hadn't even known Brent's last name, and upon seeing his business card, I hadn't made the connection.

Had Brent been opening an office in downtown Hope Mills? Could that have had something to do with his demise?

I contemplated theories until I reached Mr. Percy's office, in a Victorian home that had been renovated and rezoned for commercial office space. While Mr. Percy was a real estate agent, his realty office also managed the properties he owned, including the building which housed D'Amico's and Subplot.

As I walked into his office, he squinted at his computer screen, his small glasses resting on the tip of his nose. He typed by pecking at the keyboard with both index fingers. As soon as we made eye contact, he recognized me immediately.

"He-hey! Mr. Parker. How's it going?" He had a full head of thinning gray hair, and he wore a sage green button shirt tucked in to a pair of khakis. "Please—take a seat."

"I was just strolling through town, and I thought I'd swing by to ask a quick question." I sat down in an upholstered chair with a burgundy floral pattern that must have been in his office since at least the early nineties.

"Sure thing. How can I help?" He removed the glasses.

"I'm looking to install some security cameras throughout my lounge, and maybe add some other security measures that weren't part of the initial renovation plans you approved."

Mr. Percy's eyes widened. "Spooked by the terrible events that took place this week, eh?"

I stared into my hands, which were folded in my lap. "Yeah," I mumbled.

"I've lived in Hope Mills for my entire life. If you can't tell by looking at me, that's a long time." He paused for a beat, perhaps waiting for me to laugh, although I didn't. "It's always been such a safe, serene town. One always thinks *something like this can't happen here* until it does."

"I know. I think I'm still in shock. And to think it happened right outside of Subplot. It's horrifying. Which is why I think it's time to install some security measures. I wish I'd done it sooner, but, like you, I figured we were safe."

Not answering my query about security cameras, Mr. Percy simply said, "Brent Crestmore."

"Yep." I nodded, unsure if Mr. Percy had anything else to say on the topic.

"You know, he expressed interest in buying up some of my property."

I sat up straight. "He did? Why would he do that?"

"Crestmore Enterprises. Ever heard of it?"

"It's funny you mention that. As I was walking, I saw a storefront with a Crestmore Enterprises sign in the window. Was he looking to build his office in one of your properties?"

Mr. Percy chuckled and crossed one leg over his other. "Not quite. He was a real estate developer, and he owns stake in tons of businesses—from bars and restaurants to hospitality. He goes to small towns like ours with high tourist potential and swoops in to grow his business footprint there. He was about to make me an offer I couldn't refuse for some of my properties. That storefront you passed will probably be filled by some small chain restaurant from his portfolio."

"Would you have sold to him?" I asked.

"Well, I guess it's not very relevant now. Who knows what will happen to his business since he called all the shots." He snatched a pen from his desktop and clicked it repeatedly in his hand. "But he was about to make a very strong offer, and I'm getting up there in years. I don't know if I'll be doing this much longer." His answer was noncommittal, but he made it sound like moving forward with the deal was in the cards.

If Mr. Percy had sold the building where D'Amico's and Subplot were located, it was possible Brent wouldn't have renewed our leases. In that case, we could've been forced out, only for him to bring in businesses from his portfolio.

Though I hadn't been aware of Crestmore Enterprises and Brent's business dealings for long, could they have given me an apparent motive through the eyes of the police?

"But there I go on one of my tangents." Mr. Percy laughed. "Go ahead and install the security cameras. If you're doing anything to the locks, I only ask that you keep me in the loop so that I can access the space when I need to for utility purposes."

"Thank you so much. I'll fill you in on any details."

We chatted for a few more minutes, talking about the beautiful spring weather. Though I wasn't an avid sports spectator, I fumbled my way through a brief conversation about baseball that he'd initiated, including how he'd be taking his young grandchildren to their first Philadelphia home game over the weekend.

However, for the rest of our conversation and after I left, my mind became a factory for theories about how Brent's death might have been related to Crestmore Enterprises.

If any business owners in town were aware of Brent's ploy to buy up property in Hope Mills, force out small businesses, only to replace them with chains he had investments in, they could've had motive.

I first thought about my upstairs neighbor Heidi. If Kristin had been honest and accurate in saying that she and Brent had argued before the Lifted Spirits tasting, could their altercation have been related to Brent's business intentions?

Mr. Percy was open with me about Brent's potential offer, and Heidi often bragged about her strong relationship with our landlord. Because D'Amico's had been in his property for decades, I wondered if he would've clued Heidi in before the fact. Heidi could be cold under normal circumstances, so how would she treat someone she knew could be an active threat to her family restaurant?

Luckily, it wasn't hard for me to run into Heidi. The next time I saw her, I planned to ask her some questions to decipher how much she knew.

And although it was a stretch, the other business owner my mind went to was Logan. Who was his landlord? Could they have filled him in on Brent's plans? Brent also had harsh words to say about DCDC. Was there a chain distillery in Brent's portfolio that he sought to bring in to Logan's space?

Though these questions and suspicions were nothing more than theories based on the limited information I had, knowing more about Brent's business dealings gave me a solid direction for the questions I needed to ask next.

FOURTEEN

With a few hours remaining before I needed to begin prep work for our Friday night service, which tended to be the busiest night of the week, I decided to walk to my parents' house. I figured it couldn't hurt to do something for my leisure which might take my mind off the murder for a while.

Despite my uneasiness, I did my best to revel in the comfortable outside air. I took off the hoodie I'd been wearing and tied it around my waist since it was finally warm enough to walk around in a T-shirt and jeans. An occasional cool breeze sent shivers down my spine when I passed through a patch of shade, but I was perfectly content when in the warmth of direct sunlight.

My parents' home was located along the Delaware Canal Towpath trail, which cut through the heart of town and extended nearly sixty miles in total. I stepped along the narrow red-dirt path parallel to the canal, which was glossed over with thick moss, yielding to cyclists as they approached or passed.

When I reached their house, I veered off the trail and sauntered through the lush green grass of their backyard. I remembered riding my bike along the trail as a child, pretending I was

on the run in a cat-and-mouse chase. *They'll never find me here!*
I'd proclaim as I zipped through the yard and imagined I was
hiding out in the garage.

I rang the doorbell once I reached the front porch. After
about thirty seconds with no response, I rang the doorbell again
and rapped on the yellow fiberglass front door.

Where could they be? I hadn't considered my parents might
be grocery shopping, out for a hike, eating lunch downtown, or
any other activity a retired couple could enjoy on a gorgeous
Friday afternoon.

I fished the ring of keys out of my pocket and grasped the
one in a yellow rubber cover which matched the front door. As I
inserted the key into the lock, their car pulled into the
driveway.

"What have you guys been up to?" I asked as they walked
up the stone-paved walkway toward the house, both dressed in
athletic clothes.

"Your father and I had a lovely afternoon playing pickleball." My mom latched on to my dad's side and patted his round
stomach. "We had a ton of fun. Didn't we, dear?"

Streams of sweat trickled down my dad's face. "Yeah. Loads
of it." His expression was deadpan.

She lifted a hand to the corner of her mouth and whispered,
"Don't worry about him. He's just a sore loser. I guess you could
say I pickled him."

My dad rolled his eyes. "Hey, I was facing the sun the entire
time."

"Yeah, yeah, yeah. Excuses, excuses." She released her grip
on him, clasping both palms to her cheeks. "You'll never guess
who we saw there."

"Oh, come on, Stace. We don't have to talk about this now."

"Who?" I asked.

"Maybe we better go inside first," she replied.

I followed my parents into the house, down the hallway, and to the open kitchen and dining room. I took a seat on one of the tall bar chairs behind the island as my mom removed eggs, vegetables, mushrooms, and cheese from the refrigerator. My dad sat alone at the dining room table behind me.

"Who wants an omelet?" my mom asked. My dad and I each gave our hands a slight raise, and she took note of both of our reactions. "Three omelets coming right up."

"Who did you see at the pickleball courts?" I asked again. If I hadn't, I knew they would've carried on as if my mom hadn't brought it up in the first place.

She began to chop a green pepper. "It was Chloe."

"Did you chat with her at all?"

My dad fidgeted with the woven placemat in front of him. "We don't have to get into it."

"I'm sorry I brought it up," my mom said in a sulking tone. She reached for a shiitake mushroom, not looking up at my dad and me as she prepared to chop it.

"Chloe and I aren't on bad terms. We're actually planning to meet up soon and talk."

My mom put her chef's knife down on the counter and glanced up at me. "Really?" She beamed. "Do you think you two can patch things up?"

Here comes the inevitable plea for grandchildren.

My dad sighed and pinched the bridge of his nose.

I scratched at my stubbly beard. "There's nothing to be patched up. We respect each other, and we still want to be a part of one another's lives."

"I guess I just don't understand how you'd want to be in each other's lives but not get married."

"We can be friends."

"Why won't you share what went wrong?"

I couldn't find the words to respond.

I wanted so badly to come out in that moment, but I also wanted to tell my parents the truth during a positive conversation, not in the midst of tension. I wanted to come out on my own terms, not in response to my mom's questions.

The open kitchen and dining room sunk into silence, except for the sound of my mom cracking eggs into a glass bowl.

"So, how are things going with the case?" my dad interjected, officially changing the subject.

I briefly filled them in on the wallet we'd discovered the night before and what I'd learned about Brent earlier in the day, including my conversation with Mr. Percy.

After my mom finished cooking and each of us ate our omelets stuffed with ham, green peppers, mushrooms, spinach, and feta, I excused myself to head to Subplot.

Although I was nervous about how my parents—especially my mom—would react to my coming out, I ultimately trusted that I'd have their support. I believed their largest hurdle would be reconciling who I was with the vision they had for who they hoped I'd become.

I wanted my parents to know the full truth about me. I hoped it could bring us closer together, even if it would take time.

I just needed to find the courage to tell them—another day, of course.

As I strode down Main Street on my way to work for the evening, I spotted a flowerbed filled with bright red tulips. They reminded me of strawberries, and it sparked an idea to craft a strawberry-rhubarb gin fizz cocktail I could potentially add to our upcoming summer menu.

Late-nineties alternative music grew louder as I approached Ampersand, a relatively new bookstore in Hope Mills.

As I gazed into the shop, I held my breath as I spotted the beautiful worker I'd been crushing on. I didn't know him by name, but I surely knew his face. His rich, milk chocolate brown eyes locked with mine as he glanced briefly out the window, mere feet away. His medium-length, wavy, sun-streaked hair was parted on the left side of his head in a way that made me want to run my fingers through it.

A few weeks before, I was on a similar walk down Main Street as an April shower let loose. I'd picked up my pace to rush back to Subplot without getting drenched, and the worker popped out of the shop to pull a cart of used books from the sidewalk inside.

Ever since, I kept an eye out for him any time I wandered by Ampersand.

He wore a plain white T-shirt with the sleeves rolled up, exposing his toned biceps and triceps with strong veins snaking up his forearms.

Although I'd only admired him from a distance, I frequently contemplated stopping into the store to browse so I might get a chance to learn his name or talk to him, although I wasn't sure I could keep my cool if I did.

And so I kept moseying down Main Street.

As badly as I wanted to introduce myself, it was too soon to be thinking about crushes and dating while I healed from the broken engagement and sought to discover myself in the ruins. Plus, considering I'd never had a romantic experience with a guy before, it felt like a giant leap.

"Reece?" Chloe's unmistakable soft voice rang out behind me. The same voice I'd heard laugh, cry, tell jokes, support my dreams, and occasionally scold me for leaving dirty socks lying around. "Is that you?"

My heart raced, and I spun around on the sidewalk.

Not now.

Her timing was uncanny. Standing between Chloe and my recently-discovered crush on the sidewalk outside of Ampersand was like being cornered by my past as I dreamed about what my future might look like one day. I knew it was up to my present self to work through the difficult situation if I planned to move forward.

I let out a dejected sigh before turning around. "Hey, Chlo." I tried to sound excited, despite my internal freaking out. "What are you up to?"

I couldn't help but grin as I caught a glimpse of her silky hair cascading over each shoulder like a golden waterfall. She carried a paper box from Jackie and Jill's Bakery on one palm while resting her other hand on top to keep it level. "It's our executive chef's fiftieth birthday today, so I had a cake made. The whole restaurant is going to surprise him when he comes in for his shift later."

We exchanged pleasantries, and I gave her a one-armed, awkward hug to accommodate her full hands.

After stepping apart from our hug, she said, "I saw your parents earlier when I was playing pickleball with some friends."

I tsked. "Yeah, I heard. I just left my parents' house. My mom told me all about it. Sorry if they made things awkward."

She waved off my concern. "Oh, stop it. You know I adore them." Her eyes widened, and she raised her eyebrows as if she'd had a sudden realization. "I almost forgot to ask. Did you hear the news?"

"News? About what? Did they figure out who killed Brent?"

The way she jerked her head closer to me, almost as if trying to make herself look small, made me anticipate a big revelation.

She glanced in all directions, perhaps to make sure no one was within earshot. "Kristin Marshall has gone missing."

FIFTEEN

"Kristin?" I nearly choked on a gasp. "As in …?"

"She's a borough councilwoman. Based on what I overheard from Cam, it sounds like she might be connected to the murder case."

"She did make some pretty aggressive remarks toward the guy who ended up dead."

My mind flashed back to my brief encounter with Kristin that morning. We'd locked eyes as she sped out of Brent's driveway.

Could she have disappeared as a result of me spotting her in a place she shouldn't have been? If that was the case, though, she hadn't vanished for a full twenty-four hours, which meant she couldn't have been officially missing. Or was she simply avoiding the police? Was she on the run?

I took a step backward and nearly lost my balance. "I figured you were talking about her. But how do you …?"

"Cam filled me in on the investigation. They haven't been able to locate or reach her."

"He did? I thought the details would be confidential."

"Well, technically he didn't *tell* me. But he stopped by my parents' house this morning, and he stepped aside to take a phone call, which I *might* have eavesdropped on." Chloe had moved back to her parents' house while I finished up the lease in our shared apartment before moving into a smaller apartment of my own.

"Chloe!" I exclaimed, equally relieved, excited, and cautious.

"I know, I know. I shouldn't have been listening in," she said with an exhausted sigh and an eye roll. "So, this is your warning to be careful about how you use that information. I could get into big trouble, and not just with Cam."

"Why would you share this with me, then?"

"Because you found the victim's body and it happened right outside your lounge. The detective and her team are continuing to investigate in multiple directions, and I know you couldn't have done it. If you're trying to clear yourself from any suspicion, I thought it might be helpful information."

How was I supposed to use the intel from Chloe without making it obvious I'd learned it from her?

Be grateful, I told myself.

"Well, thanks for telling me. I just ..." I couldn't formulate another word as my mind raced. "I hope she's not in any danger —or worse." I shuddered at the thought. "I just saw her this morning—very briefly."

Her eyes widened. "You did? It sounded to me like she hadn't been reachable since yesterday. Where did you see her?"

An emptiness grew in the pit of my stomach. "I might have driven past the victim's house this morning. He lived in a massive farmhouse on the outskirts of town. When I drove by, a car flew down the driveway, and she was driving."

Chloe grimaced. "You should absolutely share that with the police. It sounds like an important detail."

"I will," I whispered, mindful that we were chatting on

Main Street and someone could walk by at any moment. "But can you please keep this between us until I do?"

If Kristin had been missing since the day before, I doubted she was under duress by Brent's killer, although it could've been possible. When I'd seen her, she seemed to be on her own.

Was she on the run to escape suspicion by the authorities? That'd be dumb. Detective Sharp had been very direct when she told me leaving Hope Mills given the circumstances would look mighty suspicious. However, if Kristin was guilty, she might not be thinking or acting rationally.

Was it possible Kristin went missing on purpose, to deflect blame or appear like a victim or escape questioning?

Either way, the fact Kristin couldn't be located or reached added a new layer of complexity to the case.

"And that's not all," Chloe continued.

"There's more?"

"Mm-hmm." She snuck a quick peek over each of her shoulders again. "On the same phone call, Cam mentioned evidence found at the crime scene. Although his wallet had been missing, the victim had a receipt from D'Amico's restaurant in his pocket, and the restaurant's owner was listed as the server on it. According to the receipt, the victim had one drink at D'Amico's. I'm not sure why that's important, but there you go."

Had Heidi served Brent alcohol, after all? If her name was printed on his receipt, then I questioned her credibility, since she was adamant he hadn't had any drinks at D'Amico's. Could that drink have contained a fatal substance?

I allowed my hands to fall from my hips as my arms hung at my side. "At least there's *some* evidence pointing to someone other than me. I wish none of this happened in the first place, though."

"He mentioned another piece of evidence, too. Something about a business card from the distillery guy in the victim's pocket. Apparently, there was some sort of cryptic note scribbled on it."

Logan.

"Did you catch anything about what the note said?"

"No. Unfortunately, that's all I heard. I wanted to warn you since you work around the owner of D'Amico's and the guy from the distillery. And if you can use that intel to clear your name ..." Chloe squinted one eye and leaned in closer. "But remember, you heard *none* of this from me."

I filled my cheeks with air and let my lips vibrate as they deflated. "This is a lot to process."

"I know. I'm sharing this information purely for your safety and because I know deep down you couldn't have killed someone. That much I'm sure of without a doubt. So, I need to be able to trust you won't blow my cover for sharing sensitive information."

"You can trust me, Chlo." While I wanted to do some further investigating to look into Heidi and Logan, I needed to be extra careful to not tarnish her belief in me. The last thing I wanted was for her to be in hot water because she tried to help me.

Chloe's phone dinged, and she read a message on her smart watch. "Shoot. I have to run, but do you have some time to get together this weekend? I think we should talk ... about other stuff," she said, likely referring to our breakup.

As much as I dreaded the conversation, I owed her my time and attention, and I wanted to make sure she found closure in the aftermath of our relationship. However, with the stress of the murder investigation, I didn't have much mental space to deal with my deepest, darkest feelings.

"Oh, uh ... yeah." Already, I could tell she was disappointed by my less-than-enthusiastic response. I hated feeling like I was continually letting her down. "How about tomorrow? I know tomorrow would've been ..."

Chloe swatted away a fly buzzing around her. "Sure. Tomorrow works for me. Could you meet up at ten? We can meet at the pocket park you mentioned."

"Sounds great." There'd be no backing out of our meetup, especially considering all the valuable information she'd shared —most of which should've been kept secret.

We exchanged see-you-laters and a one-armed hug.

After she continued on her way, I wandered over to a nearby bench and relished the cool breeze brushing over my skin as I sat. With eyes closed, I visualized everything I knew about the case as if I was a private investigator in a movie—with pictures and evidence taped to my wall with red yarn and thumbtacks making some sense out of the chaos.

Thinking about how Brent's receipt from D'Amico's included one alcoholic beverage, I immediately became suspicious of Heidi and Kristin. If what Chloe shared was true, they both either lied or embellished the truth. And where there were lies, there were secrets.

Kristin had been adamant that Heidi overserved Brent. But if the receipt truly revealed Brent only had one drink at D'Amico's, then it looked like Kristin was trying to redirect suspicion.

But given her disappearance, I couldn't decide whether I was more or less convinced she had something to do with Brent's murder.

On the other hand, Heidi claimed she and her staff hadn't served Brent a drop of alcohol. While the receipt didn't show she'd overserved him as Kristin claimed, it did prove she was lying. What did she have to gain from lying, especially considering that one alcoholic beverage wouldn't have been enough to push Brent over the edge? If she was somehow aware of Brent's intentions to buy up property and bring in his own businesses to Hope Mills, was she lying to disguise darker intentions?

And what about the business card found in Brent's pocket?

When Chloe said the card was from the "distillery guy," I felt almost certain she meant Logan. And the cryptic note scribbled on it—what could it have said?

Heidi had mentioned seeing Ava and Logan arguing before the estimated time of murder, though I questioned her reliability after learning she'd lied about serving Brent alcohol.

But then there was also Will's observation of Ava's frantic phone call. And she'd found Brent's wallet. Perhaps I was getting ahead of myself, but was it possible Ava could've staged finding the wallet? What if she'd had it all along? Or could Logan have had something to do with it?

Though I'd been hesitant to suspect Ava of any wrongdoing, I no longer felt so sure she was innocent if Logan was a suspect. After all, Logan had been in the lounge that night, too.

If they were indeed having an argument on the night Brent died, could it have been about killing him or what to do with his body? Could Ava and Logan have carried out the murder together?

I didn't want to consider those two had anything to do with Brent's death, but I had no choice.

I wasn't only eager to find out *who* killed Brent. I needed to know *why*.

SIXTEEN

Ava arrived at Subplot through our bookcase entrance as I sifted through a stack of mail, invoices, and other paperwork at the bar.

Regardless of my recent suspicions about her, I hoped with all my heart she wasn't connected to Brent's murder. She'd been my right-hand person at multiple bars before Subplot. We'd always had each other's backs, whether dealing with a difficult customer, being supportive during a breakup, or giving honest feedback. The bar and restaurant biz could be fickle, but Ava was the one constant in my career.

However, her odd behavior and the few pieces of gossip I'd heard about her leading up to that evening's shift made me question her innocence, and I hated it.

Innocent or guilty, suspicious or not, I cared about Ava and wanted the best for her and her career.

I sat at the bar with my laptop open as I crunched some numbers and updated our bookkeeping. While getting any new business off the ground was a challenge, the numbers always made my head spin. And not only because math was never my strongest subject—but because Subplot still had quite some way to go before it was profitable given the large investment it took up front to open it.

"How have you been hanging in there?" I asked Ava with the best of intentions as she prepared for a busy Friday night.

"Honestly, it's been super hard," she answered as she chopped a large, juicy lime into wedges and loaded them into a fruit dispenser on top of the bar. "I haven't been sleeping well at all. I get the police are doing their jobs by speaking with all of us, but I hate feeling like I'm under a microscope. It's like they're waiting for us to say something sketchy. Or like they're coaxing us to confess to something, even if it isn't true."

While it was a reasonable concern, I wondered if Ava's apprehension was rooted in something darker. "What could you possibly have to confess, though? I'm sure they're using psychological tactics to gather as much information as they can."

"I don't know." She stalled and grabbed another lime to chop. She remained focused as she slid the knife back and forth to cut the fruit in half, as if she was afraid it might slip from her hands. "And besides, Hope Mills is such a small town, and it's scary to think there's someone among us who could do such a cruel thing. It's even more terrifying to consider we were around for some of Brent's final moments. Not only does it make anyone who was here the other night look suspicious, but it gives the killer reason to hurt us."

"What do you mean?" I pushed my laptop aside to give Ava my full attention.

"I'm concerned the killer will retaliate against witnesses for sharing information with the police. I mean, the body was found behind the lounge. And his wallet showed up here. It seems like we're being framed."

Her concern was valid. If the killer was on the loose, they

might be taking active steps to steer the police's attention or prevent potential witnesses from speaking out.

I couldn't stop fidgeting with one of the invoices in front of me as I considered her perspective. "You have a point about retaliation. I heard a rumor today about Kristin from Lifted Spirits. Apparently, she was reported missing." I intentionally didn't mention my sighting, not wanting to sway her response.

Ava froze mid-way through slicing a lime and gently laid the knife on the bar. "Shut up. See! She probably knew something important about the case, spoke up to police, and now who knows what terrible things are being done to her."

Her concern about revenge also piqued my suspicion of Logan. Because they'd allegedly been together on the night of the murder, did she know something that made him look guilty? And if so, was she fearful he might hurt her if she didn't keep quiet?

I hesitated to mention Logan, worried I might scare her from sharing more, but I felt like it was my duty to make sure Ava wasn't at risk. What if *she* was a victim in all of this?

"This might sound like it's coming out of nowhere, but I promise I'm only asking out of concern."

She grasped the edge of the bar as if to steady herself and turned toward me to give her undivided attention. "What is it?"

"You know Logan, right?"

She removed the vinyl gloves she'd been wearing while she prepped the fruit and swayed ever so slightly. "From the distillery? Of course I know him. And speaking of DCDC, we're running low on the new bourbon. We should have enough to last us through the end of this weekend, but we're due to place an order soon."

"And what do you think of him?" I mentally filed her comment about inventory away for later.

Ava crossed her arms over her chest. "He's a nice guy. I

don't know him very well, though." She rocked forwards and backwards on her heels. "What does that have to do with anything?"

"I heard a rumor around town. Do you know if the police are suspicious of him at all?"

"Not that I'm aware, but he was here the night Brent was found." She shrugged and frowned dismissively. "I'm trying to steer clear of any gossip about the case."

I forced out a laugh and swiped my palm as if to say, *Never mind*. "You know how rumors can spread in a small town."

I considered ending the conversation there, but I knew I wouldn't be able to sleep if I didn't travel down all avenues to make sure Ava was safe. "Someone said they saw you and Logan together after you left the lounge on the night of the murder. They said it looked like you two were arguing."

Ava's eyelids fluttered. "What? No. We weren't. And besides, how is this relevant at all?"

"Because I'm worried about you. If there was something going on between you, I just wanted to make sure you're not in any danger since I've heard some talk about him."

She shook her head slowly and stared at the glossy, varnished bar. "Yes, I was with Logan. We weren't doing anything wrong, I swear. It had nothing to do with Brent." She paused, looking like she was about to say something, but only stuttered for a few seconds.

I wanted to mention Logan's business card was found in Brent's pocket after he'd passed, but I couldn't betray Chloe's trust. And besides, if Cam found out I'd shared potentially classified information, I was sure to be in hot water for interfering with the investigation. So, instead, I tried to probe one more time. "And you're sure he didn't do anything ... off? He's not the one making you paranoid about retaliation, is he? I promise you can trust me."

Ava inhaled and exhaled deeply. "No …" Her voice was light, airy, and unconvincing.

My gut told me she wasn't telling the whole story. I speculated whether she knew something more and was too afraid to tell me—or if she was somehow involved herself and trying to cover her tracks.

The cocktail lounge opened at six, as usual. On a typical Friday night, customers arrived at a steady pace from six to eight, putting us at or near capacity. However, once eight o'clock hit— particularly on a Friday—our small space couldn't keep up with the demand.

Luckily, Lainey did a great job of managing our waitlist, and we'd gotten into a tight rhythm of communication in the preceding weeks. When Dante, Ava, or I delivered a check to a table preparing to leave, we used our earpiece walkie talkies to let her know we'd be ready for another party soon. From there, she'd use our digital waitlist app to text the next customer in the queue. By the time they arrived back to Lainey's maître d' stand, Dante had the previous party's area cleared and wiped down.

I approached a man and woman who appeared to be a couple at the end of the bar to take their order. They were in the middle of a conversation when I overheard the man say, "And now they can't find Kristin Marshall—she's on borough council. Some guys at work heard she might have something to do with all of this."

I crouched down behind the bar, pretending to organize bottles so I could listen, instead of interrupting their conversation.

The woman sighed. "Or maybe she's next. Gosh, I hope not."

I stood at full posture and approached the couple to greet them and take their order.

"We'll have one Huckleberry Gin and one Green Gables, please," the woman ordered for the two of them.

I crafted their beverages right in front of them, but their conversation about Kristin had tapered off.

Huckleberry Gin proved to be one of the most popular cocktails of the spring season, and I was glad Green Gables—a tequila-based cocktail featuring matcha and mint—got some love.

I filled a shaker with ice, tequila, coconut milk, honey, and two sprigs of fresh mint, pounded the lid firmly on the shaker, and lifted it above my shoulder.

As I began to shake the beverage, the high-pitched wail of a fire alarm swelled through Subplot. Strobe lights from every corner flashed, illuminating the room in bright white for a half-second at a time.

I jolted and lost grip of the shaker, causing it to crash on the bar and soak the front of my shirt. My already-racing heart beat harder and faster.

The lounge quickly descended into chaos as everyone covered their ears to protect them from the shrill alarm. Customers yelled over the alarm to communicate with their groups as they reached for their belongings and debated what to do with their beverages.

I jogged around the front of the bar and did my best to project my voice over the alarm and all the other commotion. "Everyone, please follow me out this emergency exit!" I ran over to the metal exit door I'd avoided at all costs since finding Brent's body, except to take out the trash.

Quickly, a line formed, and everyone filtered out the door and into the alley behind the lounge as I held it open.

"Do you smell smoke?" one customer asked another as they exited.

"No, I don't ..."

Others craned their necks upon leaving the building.

"It doesn't look like it's on fire."

"Maybe it was something in the kitchen upstairs?"

"Are we supposed to wait around until this is all cleared so we can pay our tab?" another customer asked as they trickled out of the lounge.

As I held the heavy metal door open for customers to evacuate, I couldn't resist feeling like I was being targeted yet again.

With this chaos taking place at Subplot each night since the murder, maybe Ava was right to be concerned about retaliation.

SEVENTEEN

"Is everyone out?" Ava asked, standing beside me as I held open the downstairs exit door to evacuate our customers from Subplot.

"I think so." I poked my head into the lounge to make sure no one lingered behind. The only thing inside were the white flashing strobe lights and the reverberating echo of the ear-piercing fire alarm.

"All clear?"

"Yep. I didn't see anyone else in there." I turned to face the group of customers lingering in the alley.

I winced as they rubbernecked at the yellow tape still stretched around the crime scene. Some of the customers carried their cocktails with them. Although it wasn't permitted, I took it as a compliment that they'd salvage our cocktails from a burning building. An array of battery-powered flameless candles in green glass votive jars and a few bouquets of flowers were arranged just outside the caution tape. Despite how difficult Brent had been during the Lifted Spirits tasting and despite all the enemies he seemed to have garnered, my heart sunk as I considered Brent's loved ones.

I cleared my throat as I prepared to speak up. "I'm so sorry about this, everyone. If you could please follow me, I'd like to get us as far away from the building as we can until the fire department says we're all clear."

The group of approximately two dozen customers followed me down the narrow gravel alleyway and past the dumpster where I'd found Brent. "Watch your step. It's a bit uneven." We stepped carefully in the dark as we reached the end of the alley and turned down a narrow cement sidewalk toward Main Street which led us to the front of the building.

As the fire alarm screaming inside D'Amico's and Subplot grew fainter, a fire truck's siren shrieked as it approached, punctuated with several hard blasts of its deep horn. Soon, the darkness was flooded with flashing red and white lights.

Though my primary focus was set on making sure everyone —from both Subplot and D'Amico's—was alright and our building wasn't in jeopardy, I couldn't help but wonder what triggered the alarm. Had something caught fire in the kitchen at D'Amico's? Did someone pull the fire alarm to disrupt or distract from the investigation?

"Reece. Is that you?" Heidi's angry voice yelled in the distance before she marched in my direction. "What's this all about?"

I tilted my head and squinted at her. It was so hard to focus with flashing lights and the commotion of a shocked crowd of customers from both of our businesses surrounding us. I tried to respond as calmly as possible since many people in the small crowd filmed the scene around us, presumably to share on social media. "I don't know what set off the alarm. Was everything alright in your kitchen?"

My question was sincere, but one would've thought I slapped Heidi across the face by how loudly she scoffed.

"You're blaming *me?* There was no fire in my restaurant.

How rude of you to insinuate there would be so much as a burnt meatball coming from my kitchen."

I sighed, exhausted. I wanted to stand up to her, but I didn't have the energy to try to make a point. "Maybe the fire alarm malfunctioned."

"Well, I think someone pulled it." She crossed her arms. "It would make sense considering all the *unsavory* behavior going on in your cocktail lounge this week. I'd say a malfunction"—she used air quotes as she said that last word—"of the alarm system would be a rather convenient explanation, don't you think?"

Rather than try to reason with her, I closed my eyes and inhaled a deep breath. The air was tinged with the scent of freshly mowed grass, but I couldn't detect even the slightest hint of smoke, so I hoped a malfunction was the simple explanation for the evening's disruption.

"Mr. Parker." A familiar woman's voice tore me out of my brief meditation. "Ms. D'Amico."

Opening my eyes, I saw Detective Sharp.

Despite the queasiness I felt in her presence, I pasted on a smile. "Oh, hi, Detective."

"What are you doing here?" Heidi wailed before burying her face in her hands.

The detective fished her field notebook and tiny pen from an interior pocket of her jacket, a ritual which was becoming all too familiar to me. "I heard the fire department was dispatched here on my scanner. Given the events that unfolded here a couple of nights ago, I figured I'd make sure nothing suspicious is going on. We can't be too careful."

Heidi crossed her arms. "Well, in that case, I'm glad you're here. I'm sick of all this nefarious behavior, so I hope you can get to the bottom of it."

"While we wait for the firefighters to give us the all-clear, do either of you care to share anything out of the ordinary you witnessed tonight?" the detective asked without acknowledging her melodrama, which sent a pang of satisfaction through me.

"Tonight was as normal as could be, Detective," Heidi answered in a sugary-sweet, clearly fake tone before Detective Sharp finished asking the question.

I paused to reflect on the evening, but nothing noteworthy or suspicious stood out in my mind. "It felt like an ordinary Friday night to me."

"Right," the detective commented. Her casual tone made it seem like she didn't believe either of us. "You see, it strikes me as odd that someone was murdered outside of your shared building on Wednesday, the victim's wallet was discovered in your building on Thursday, and now the fire department is dispatched to a scene where there are no obvious signs of fire on Friday. Your building is the epicenter of a variety of bad behavior lately."

"You're so right, Detective. I expressed the same concerns to Reece before you arrived." Heidi planted both of her clenched fists on each of her hips and scowled at me as if to say, *I told you so.*

Detective Sharp harrumphed. "That's enough, Ms. D'Amico. I'm talking to you, too. We haven't ruled out your involvement in this case either."

Ha!

Delighted as I was to know I wasn't alone in the police's ring of suspicion—and equally glad the detective put Heidi in her place—it scared me to consider Brent's potential killer could be working right upstairs and someone I interacted with almost daily. With the information I'd learned from Mr. Percy in mind, I considered her potential motive and shivered at the prospect Heidi might've pulled the fire alarm. Could she have done it to point blame toward me? I reminded myself to tread carefully with her.

"Detective," a man's raspy voice called out from over my shoulder, prompting Heidi and me to turn around. A firefighter in a full tan, black, and neon green uniform approached us, carrying his helmet at his side. "The building is all clear. We've confirmed the fire alarm was triggered manually by one of the wall-mounted fire alarm pull stations in the restaurant upstairs. We'll have the report available soon your department can refer to."

As the firefighter walked away, Heidi and I both sheepishly faced the detective again.

"Manually triggering a fire alarm when there is no fire is a fineable offense. I guess this will be added to the list of illegal activities I'm investigating," the detective said.

"Can we let our customers back into the building now?" Heidi whined. "We're going to have to cook so many meals again, and I'm sure some people left without paying their tabs. We're going to lose money on this for sure."

Detective Sharp's eyes flicked toward the sky and shook her head ever so slightly. "Not yet."

"What?" Heidi retorted.

"I'd like the three of us to do a building walkthrough. Given what's happened here over the past few days, I'd like the two of you to make sure nothing is glaringly suspicious or out of place."

I agreed with the detective's idea. What if the fire alarm gave an assailant the opportunity to plant or remove evidence?

We followed the detective into D'Amico's and surveyed the dining room with half-eaten plates of pasta at almost every place setting. We went through the restaurant's kitchen, office, supply closet, and two all-gender restrooms.

I'd fully expected Heidi to point out a minor detail in order to shirk suspicion or make herself appear to be a victim in the ordeal, but she didn't. "Nothing seems out of place to me," she said.

As we stepped down the hallway after checking both restrooms, a sliver of brown leather caught my eye. The object nearly blended in with the restaurant's laminate flooring that resembled dark mahogany.

"Wait a second." I crouched down and squinted at the bracelet as it came into view. "I've seen this before."

"What? What did you find?" Heidi's voice grew louder as she hurried across the room to get a closer look.

"Please don't touch anything," Detective Sharp instructed.

I lifted my hands on either side of my head, making it clear I hadn't laid a finger on it.

My mouth hung open. "This bracelet. It's Kristin's! Maybe that means she's not missing after all."

"How do you ...?"

I interrupted the detective's question, feeling certain about what she'd ask. "Kristin approached me at the Roastery the other day. I specifically noticed this bracelet, and I complimented her on it. There's a raccoon charm on it, and I love raccoons." From my crouched position below the fire alarm, I gazed up at Heidi and Detective Sharp. "I heard she's been missing, but could she have pulled the alarm?"

Heidi gasped. "I knew it. I knew she had something to do with this. And it'd be just like her to stage a disappearance to avoid complying with the authorities." She placed both hands on her hips and let out a disgusted grunt.

Detective Sharp shifted her position, raising a palm at both of us. "Whoa, whoa, whoa. At this stage, we have no way of knowing if she could've done this." She paused, but her lips kept moving, and I could see her eyes trying to compute a theory. "I'd say it's pretty well known that pulling a false alarm comes with consequences. Now, let's assume Kristin staged her own disappearance. If that were the case, don't you think she'd take every precaution to leave nothing behind, especially a piece of jewelry you commented on a couple of days ago?" Her reasoning checked out.

But it also got the wheels in my head turning. "Do you think someone else could've pulled the alarm and left this behind to throw us off? If she was kidnapped or taken hostage, could her attacker have planted this?"

"It's possible," she answered.

"Wait." I sprung up to stand directly in front of the detective. "Let's assume someone put her up to this. It's a long shot, but maybe she *did* pull the alarm but intentionally left this behind."

Heidi sidestepped to form a triangle with us. "That makes no sense. Why would she do such a thing?"

"I don't know. But maybe she guessed I'd recognize this bracelet since we talked about it the other day. Maybe it's a clue so we'd know she's still around. The bracelet could be a cry for help."

Heidi squinted. "So you're saying she *did* do it, after all."

"It could be possible, but we need to stay focused on the facts." Detective Sharp hadn't ruled my idea out completely, which I took as a compliment to my logic. She took a digital camera out of the pocket of her blazer and snapped a few photos of the bracelet near the fire alarm before collecting it as evidence. "I'd still like for us to take a peek downstairs."

Before stepping down to Subplot, I flipped on our industrial overhead lights at the top of the staircase. We hustled downstairs to do a quick sweep of the empty lounge.

We scanned every nook and cranny—under coffee tables, behind the bar, the supply closet, my office, and the small kitchen.

"Besides the turned-over cocktail shaker on the bar, nothing seems odd or out of place," the detective said as I led her and Heidi toward our single restroom at the end of the hall.

I turned around and gestured at the wet spot on the front of my shirt with both hands. "Oh, I did that. The fire alarm startled me, and I lost my grip while I was making a drink." My eyes fell to the ground with mild embarrassment, hoping that detail might show the detective I had nothing to do with the false alarm.

The light in my restroom had been turned off, and it was only illuminated by the dim light of the wax warmer beside the sink as the audiobook of *The Great Gatsby* played on a Bluetooth speaker.

As the detective flipped on the restroom light, I gasped as I read the message scrawled on the mirror in what appeared to be black permanent marker: STAY AWAY REECE.

My muscles tensed and it seemed like the room was starting to spin.

"Oh my gosh! Who could have done this?" Heidi cried out in hysterics, though her voice sounded muffled to me.

I clenched my fingers around the doorframe to steady myself, wishing my lightheadedness would subside.

Whoever pulled the alarm in D'Amico's must've dropped Kristin's bracelet, headed down to Subplot, wrote a threat on my bathroom mirror, and fled out the downstairs exit after we'd all evacuated and made our way to the front of the building. It seemed like a risky feat.

Heidi glared at me. "What could you have done to invite such evil into this building?" The words sounded clearer as I regained composure.

I didn't respond.

The detective stepped out of the restroom and into the hallway.

"Ms. D'Amico, you're free to allow your customers back inside. I'll be in touch with you soon about reviewing any footage from your security cameras." Detective Sharp turned to face me with hands on her hips as Heidi exited up the stairs. "Mr. Parker, I'd like to chat with you privately."

I gulped and stayed silent, not speaking until spoken to.

Detective Sharp began to pace back and forth in front of me. "I have a hard time believing that someone would go through all this trouble to leave you a message in this way if you weren't somehow meddling in my investigation. Is there anything you'd like to share?"

I didn't have much choice but to come clean.

"My curiosity got the best of me this morning. I'd figured out where Brent lived, and I did a quick drive-by his house."

"And what were you hoping to find there?"

"I drove past, and that was it." I didn't go into any detail about wanting to learn about his profession or anything else that might explain why someone would want him dead. "I swear there was nothing else to it on my part. But when I was there, a silver car sped down his long driveway. Kristin was driving, and we made eye contact."

She pulled out her notebook and scribbled inside with her pen. "It's my job to keep this town safe. When you take matters into your own hands, it directly impacts my ability to do so—and not in a good way." She gestured toward the bathroom door down the hall. "And you're putting yourself at risk. The writing's on the wall—literally."

I broke eye contact with her, feeling ashamed for snooping around, yet excited underneath it all that I felt myself getting closer to an answer. "I'm sorry, Detective. It won't happen again."

She blew out a frustrated breath. "It better not. And if it does, I'm going to have no choice but to charge you with obstruction of justice for interfering with my investigation. Are we clear?"

I looked her in the eye again and nodded. "Yes, ma'am."

She took a long, deep breath in and out. "Now, how are you feeling? I'm sure seeing something like that on your mirror is alarming. Do you feel safe? Is anyone making you feel threatened?"

I shook my head. "I'm uneasy, but I'll be alright. And truly, thank you for looking out for all of our safety, and I'm sorry I drove by Brent's house." I opened my hand and held it out for a handshake, which she accepted. I was surprised she didn't press me further on spotting Kristin, but perhaps she had all the info she needed.

"Thank you in advance for your cooperation." The detective folded her arms. "And if even the slightest thing seems suspicious around here, I want you to give me a call. I don't care what hour of day it is or how often you call me. We need to ensure Hope Mills continues to be a safe place to call home."

EIGHTEEN

A crack of thunder reverberated through my nearly empty apartment and shocked me awake shortly after eight o'clock the next morning. With spring threatening to give way to summer, it was the first time a storm loomed over Hope Mills since the prior fall.

I'd always loved thunderstorms. While nothing could compare to a cloudless, warm sunny day, I held a special place in my heart for thunder, lightning, pouring rain, and gusts of cool wind. I found beauty in dark skies in the middle of the day, soothed by the calming white noise of rainfall.

Upon getting out of bed, I stretched and yawned before heading to the kitchen to make coffee.

As I waited for my dark roast to brew, I lamented over my bare apartment, which was in one half of a duplex house. It was a true bachelor pad. My living room was furnished with a couch, a TV on a simple stand, a half-filled bookshelf, and a stack of boxes I had yet to unpack from the move. In the kitchen, I had four of everything—plates, cups, forks, knives, spoons—and the most basic cookware. The bed I'd crawled out of was a mattress on a box spring on my bedroom floor.

I kept reminding myself my living situation was temporary —that I'd unpack all of my boxes, buy some nicer furniture, and —cliché as it sounded—begin again. However, it felt silly to establish more permanent roots until the dust settled.

While starting Subplot helped me cope, it didn't solve any of my problems. I was learning I could only outrun my feelings for so long before I had to face them head-on.

And so I decided to take some initiative as I stood on the covered porch outside the back door in my kitchen—the best thing about living in a duplex—with a steaming mug of coffee in hand as rain poured down from the heavens.

I caressed my phone in my other hand as I mustered up the courage to call Chloe. Staring at the illuminated phone screen, my chin quivered as I noticed the date—May nineteenth. Our would-be wedding day.

Even the sky is crying about it.

Our initial plan to meet in a pocket park wasn't feasible, so I called her to adjust. Knowing she was likely finishing a Saturday morning yoga session at her gym, I wondered if she'd pick up.

My heart thumped so hard it resembled the rumbling thunder as I listened to each ringing tone.

"Hey, Reece—is everything okay?" Chloe's soft voice filled my left ear.

"Good morning. Did I catch you at a bad time?" I asked, realizing I didn't answer her question.

I listened carefully for her response, sensitive to any hint of sadness in her voice. "No, not at all. I got out of yoga a couple of minutes ago, and now I'm in the car."

A sad smile tugged at my lips. *Just as I thought.*

"Reece?" There was urgency in her voice. "Is everything alright? What's going on?"

I snapped out of my moment of reflection. "Yeah, everything's fine. Why?"

"I don't know," she mumbled with a breath of relief. "Cam said someone pulled a fire alarm at your lounge yesterday, so I wasn't sure if something bad happened."

If she'd already heard about the alarm less than twelve hours since the incident had occurred, Cam must've been giving her real-time updates.

"Nah, everything's alright. It was a false alarm, thankfully. Things are as good as they can be, considering ..." I paused for a beat before getting to the purpose of my call. "I know we were planning to meet in a pocket park at ten, but this rain is intense."

"Do you still want to get together?" Chloe asked in a gentle tone which usually accompanied her sad puppy dog eyes.

"For sure. Maybe we could we meet up at Riverside Roastery instead?" I suggested.

"Sounds good to me."

"And if your brother or the detective happen to see us, we'll say it was pure coincidence." If Cam found out about my meet-up with his sister, I worried he'd stop sharing information about the investigation with her—or worse, tell the detective I was meddling.

"Psh ... I'm not worried about Cam. He's my big brother. I've got him wrapped around my finger. Does ten still work for you?"

I squinted at the time on my stove clock through the window behind me. "Sure does." That gave me about an hour and a half to prepare.

"Okay, perfect. I'm going to head home and shower and change, then I'll meet you there. Thanks for confirming."

"Awesome. See you soon."

"Bye, Reece."

"Bye."

It still felt strange to end phone calls with Chloe with a simple goodbye and no *I love you.* When we were together, we used to sign off each call saying *"Lay-tah! Love yah!"* in silly, drawn-out voices. It was one of those quirky couple's things with no clear origin or meaning. One of *our things* we'd developed over time, unique to our relationship.

Things had changed, though. While I yearned for the way things were, I knew I'd made the best decision for myself and for Chloe. I hoped I could give her some closure so we could both move on without hard hearts.

I typically would've walked to Riverside Roastery since it was less than a mile from my apartment and Hope Mills was a walkable town. But because the pouring rain would've left me a soggy mess, I drove there in my humble sedan.

Luckily, I found a parking space on the street side of the coffee shop and hurried through the front door without getting more than my hair and the tops of my shoulders wet.

I smoothed down the front of my buttercream yellow T-shirt as I approached the register to read the menu board behind the espresso bar.

"Are you trying to order without me?" Chloe teased from behind.

"Hey, hey!" As I spun around, I instinctively opened my arms, and she leaned in for a hug. The way her head nestled into my chest felt so *right.* We weren't meant to spend our lives together, but I couldn't deny the safety and comfort I felt in her familiar embrace. "Long time, no see," I added, poking fun at our recent run-in on the street.

We stepped up to the counter and exchanged greetings with the cheerful barista.

Amidst our pleasantries, a photo of Kristin on a sign which read MISSING taped to the counter in front of the register stopped me in my tracks. The flyer instructed anyone with information about her whereabouts to contact Hope Mills Police. She was a frequent customer at Riverside Roastery, and I was glad to see they were helping to get the word out.

"What can I get started for you two?" the barista asked.

"You go first," I nudged Chloe.

She ordered a lavender vanilla latte with oat milk, and I followed up to add a cold brew coffee with almond milk and a few pumps of caramel syrup.

After the barista gave us our total, I handed them my credit card. "It's on me," I told Chloe.

We stepped aside after I finished paying, and a tightness formed in my chest as I contemplated everything I wanted to tell her. Beyond worrying about what to say, I also reminded myself to listen and make sure she felt heard, although I was prepared for her to share painful feelings with me.

"Happy wedding day, I guess." Chloe started the conversation with a relaxed smile and raised mug once we sat at a circular faux marble-topped table for two in black-stained wooden chairs. We sat toward the front of the shop with a view of torrential rain soaking an empty Main Street.

My lips tightened as my heart broke all over again. "Cheers." I raised my glass to Chloe, trying to stay upbeat, but I faltered.

"Can you imagine if today had *actually* been our wedding day? I would've been a bridezilla for sure with this rain."

I furrowed my brow. "You're the most delightful person on Earth. There's no way that could've happened."

"We would've been scrambling to move the wedding indoors. It wouldn't have been pretty." She chuckled.

We'd bravely planned an outdoor ceremony on the grounds of a local vineyard and winery located a few miles from downtown, trusting the weather would hold out for us.

"Maybe it's pouring today because we *didn't* get married," I said.

"Reece, that's so sad! Don't say that."

I bowed my head. "Sorry."

"Don't apologize. You've had a difficult week."

"To say the least," I smiled nervously. "It's been ... a lot."

"Cameron's been filling me in on everything." She stared into her creamy, steaming latte.

Everything?

I allowed my shoulders to droop and puffed out a shameful breath. "I can't imagine he thinks very highly of me—and not just because I broke your heart."

"Stop it." Chloe furrowed her brow. "First of all, don't worry about my broken heart. I can take care of myself. And second, you two were great friends when we were together—and you still can be."

I watched a bead of condensation drip down the side of my glass. "But right now, I'm sure he sees me as the man who hurt his little sister. Have you told him why I ended the engagement?"

"No. I kept my word. It's not my place to out you. But trust me, deep down, I think he knows you have a good heart."

"I wish that was enough to put an end to the investigation, too. It seems like the best way to prove Subplot had nothing to do with this is to find evidence that someone else did it. I wish everything would go back to normal."

She took a sip of her latte and gave me a devious look. "If I learn anything else that might help you, I'll let you know."

"I wouldn't want you to put yourself at risk."

Chloe scoffed. "But I want to help you." She slid her hand across the table in front of me, patting it with a sincere twinkle in her eyes. "I wish you could see what other people see in you. I wish you could see what *I* see in you. I can understand how you might feel like the cards are stacked against you, but I can also tell you need to know you're supported and loved."

Although I genuinely appreciated her words of reassurance and encouragement, it hurt to remember I let such a good thing go. Would I ever find someone as supportive and compassionate as Chloe?

I realized *I* was grieving the end of our relationship. I'd broken her heart without a doubt, yet she didn't hate me. *I* was punishing myself for the decision I'd made.

A tickle formed in my throat as I fought tears from welling in my eyes. "Thanks, Chlo."

"We may not be together as a couple anymore, but I still want you in my life." She always knew the exact words that would cut directly to my core. After a long sip from her drink, she rested her mug firmly on the table. "Now that the sappy stuff's out of the way, let's make the most of this dark and stormy day."

I wiped my watering eyes with a clump of the Roastery's thin paper napkins. "Yep, enough talking about me. How have *you* been?"

"I'm doing well. I'm taking care of myself—going to yoga, working a lot, touring some apartments and houses for rent."

"Tired of living at home?" I asked with a quick chuckle. Chloe had a great relationship with her parents, but I knew how badly she must have been craving independence.

"On one hand, I don't mind eating my mom's cooking every night. On the other, I feel like I'm in high school again." She smirked. "Even leaving the house this morning, I almost told my dad I wouldn't be gone for too long ... until I remembered I'm thirty-two years old and don't have to share every detail with my parents anymore."

"Are you looking for a place closer to downtown or are you looking at the outskirts?"

Chloe lifted her mug and took a sip. "About that ..." She grimaced nervously with clenched teeth. "I've been looking at places closer to Philly. And I've considered moving down south."

"Huh?"

I couldn't envision Chloe living anywhere but Hope Mills. Like me, she'd grown up here, never left town, and became ingrained in its restaurant industry from the time she was a teenager. Although Center City, Philadelphia was an easy forty-mile drive away, the thought of her leaving never registered as a possibility in my mind. I couldn't fathom if she left the area completely.

"Yeah, I know." She crossed her arms and rubbed them with her hands, almost like she was giving herself a hug. "I think I'm ready to try something new. With the way the restaurant industry is, I could go anywhere. Everyone's short-staffed, and everyone's trying to do something new and different. As hard as this year has been, maybe our relationship ending is what I needed to discover there's a big world out there, and I still have so much yet to explore."

"Chloe, that's ..." I was at a loss for words. Of course, I'd support Chloe no matter what she did, but I was dumbfounded as I started to consider what life without her physically nearby might be like. "I'm so happy for you." A bittersweet tenderness grew in the back of my throat.

"Thanks! I'm flying down to Florida next month to tour some new places in St. Petersburg. Who knows if I'll like it, but the industry is booming down there."

Florida? Why so far?

"You're going to crush it no matter where you go." I forced out words of support in the most authentic tone I could muster, and I hoped she believed I was being genuine, as crushed as I was. She had, after all, been a glowing example of unconditional love and support.

Chloe and I enjoyed the rest of our coffee meetup, although my mind kept returning to the thought of her leaving Hope Mills.

But she deserved the same love and support she'd shown me ... and then some.

She raised her mug. "We might not be getting married, but I'd say this is a pretty nice way to spend our would-be wedding day."

I lifted my almost-empty glass toward her, and we toasted. The corners of my mouth quivered as I forced a smile. "I agree."

Rather than spending the day wallowing and worrying about Chloe, I was grateful we could find some peace on what was supposed to have been the best day of our lives.

NINETEEN

Delaware Crossing Distilling Company was in an old brick building a few doors down from Riverside Roastery. The rain had subsided to a light sprinkle, so I tested my luck by heading there on foot rather than moving my car closer.

Between Logan's business card found in Brent's pocket after he passed, his potential argument with Ava, and the likelihood he leased the building which housed DCDC, I hoped to see if and how those pieces were connected.

Along the way, I spotted more signs with Kristin's photo in plastic sheet protectors taped to telephone poles and hung in storefront windows. It was unclear whether the signs were posted by the police department or if they were created by Kristin's friends and family. As much as I hoped she wasn't in any danger, I also hated the possibility she might be on the run or staging her own disappearance to evade law enforcement.

An awning over DCDC's front door sheltered me from the sprinkles above as I tugged on the full-glass front door, dotted with blown rain. It was locked.

The hours of operation sign posted in the floor-to-ceiling

window to the right of the door showed the distillery didn't open until noon. According to my watch, it was a few minutes after eleven.

I brought both hands up to my face and shielded my peripheral vision to catch a glimpse inside the dark interior. Logan, dressed in a tight T-shirt, jeans, and cowboy boots, was behind the tasting room's small bar with six barstools in front of it, wiping it down.

Though I debated turning around and not bothering him, I couldn't resist the potential to learn new information which might tie back to Brent's murder.

I gently rapped on the glass door, causing him to jolt. He placed a hand on his chest and let out a deep breath, perhaps when he realized it was me.

"Sorry to scare you," I said after he unlocked the door and pushed it open.

"No worries, my guy. I was in a flow state. Come on in."

DCDC's tasting room was small and quaint with its wooden bar, varnished cement floors, and exposed brick walls. Bottles of gin, vodka, and bourbon were neatly arranged on shelves to the left, and branded merchandise—T-shirts, hoodies, shot glasses, cocktail shakers, and mugs—were on the right wall.

Wooden fermentation tanks, a tall copper column still, and clusters of wooden barrels were visible behind windows that filled most of the tasting room's back wall.

Logan's business cards were displayed next to the register at the end of the bar, reminding me of my purpose for visiting.

As we stood in the center of the tasting room, he removed his backward olive-green trucker hat with one hand and slicked back his wavy, golden locks with his free hand before putting it back on. "What can I do for you this fine Saturday?"

"I was just at Riverside Roastery and decided to stop by.

We're about due for some more bourbon, and I figured I'd place an order in person since I was already over here."

He snapped his fingers into finger guns. "You came at a great time, man. If you have time, I'm about to check on my fermentations and do some testing if you'd like to watch."

"I'd love to," I said, grateful for the opportunity to stick around and hopefully ask some questions.

He took down the details of my bourbon order and offered to make a delivery the next day, since I estimated we had enough to last through the end of the weekend. If for some reason we ran out, he'd reassured me he was happy to make a last-minute delivery.

"Let's head back." He waved for me to follow him.

Just outside the metal door which led to the distilling room was a sign which included details and times for educational tours. Though I'd done one before with Logan, it was fascinating to see his process in real time.

As I followed him, I squinted skeptically, watching his every move.

I'm being paranoid. He was acting perfectly normal.

"Twice a day, I need to test the pH levels, sugar content, and temperatures to make sure the mash is fermenting appropriately." The mash he mentioned was a mixture of water, yeast, and grain—which needed to contain at least fifty-one percent corn to be considered bourbon.

"It's been a wild few days in town, huh?" I asked.

He crouched down to open a tap at the bottom of the fermentation tank which allowed him to collect a sample in a glass. "It sure has."

"I don't remember anything like this ever happening in Hope Mills, and I've lived here all my life."

He snickered. "Dude. Tell me about it. No one deserves to

die that way, but you saw how that guy acted in your lounge the other night. I'm not surprised he had an enemy."

"I couldn't believe what he said about you," I interjected. "Something about going blind or worse because of your whiskey? That crossed a line. What was his deal?"

Logan stood up with the sample in a glass. "The dude was a nutcase, plain and simple. He stopped in here earlier in the week, if you can believe it."

"He did?"

Come on, Logan. Keep talking.

He picked up a digital pH meter from a small round table beside the fermentation tank. "Yep. He came in here and asked a ton of ultra-specific questions about my distilling process. Then he went on a diatribe about how he's from Kentucky and has friendships with some of the top distillers in the world and how I wouldn't know the first thing about distilling proper whiskey. It was strange though, because by the end of the conversation, he was talking like he wanted to buy me out. He even took one of my business cards."

There was the golden nugget of information I was looking for.

"Buy you out? Wouldn't that be a good thing for you?"

He recorded the pH reading in a notebook and rested the digital meter on the table. "Financially, yeah. But I've been very particular about every choice I've made for DCDC, from the design of the space to the quality of our product to the specifics of the distillation process. It's clear Brent wasn't a fan of how I run things, and I don't think I'd be willing to compromise my vision. But it gets worse."

I cocked my head to the side.

"The police found one of my business cards in that dolt's pocket when he turned up dead, so they're keeping a close eye on me."

"What?" My voice echoed throughout the distillation room. Perhaps I'd interjected a bit too loudly in my attempt to disguise I'd already heard that tidbit from Chloe. I was glad she'd proven to be a reliable source. I hoped my overcompensation didn't make Logan suspect I knew more than I let on.

"And you'll never believe this." He crossed his arms and leaned toward me. "The doofus wrote the words *OWES MONEY* on my business card in big, capital letters. So, the police think I owed him money and bumped him off to avoid paying my debts." He grunted, sending a shiver down my spine. "I've had to go through my bookkeeping to prove I've never had a transaction with him."

Did Logan actually owe Brent? And even if he could prove he didn't have any debts to Brent on the books, was it possible they had cut some sort of deal under the table?

"And that's all he wrote on the card with no other context?" I asked.

Logan sighed. "Yep. That's all it said, besides a strange scribble above the note. He must've had trouble getting his pen to write."

He picked up another digital instrument that looked like a syringe used to give an injection.

I pointed at it in his hand. "What does that do?"

"This is a specific gravity—or SG—meter. It helps me measure the sugar content in the mash. Fermentation causes the sugar to convert to alcohol and carbon dioxide, so measuring the sugar content shows me how far along the fermentation process is. The whole batch could be ruined if the process ends too quickly, so it's important to keep an eye on the sugar content to help us rectify any potential issues."

I asked a few follow-up questions about his process before subtly pivoting the conversation back to Brent. "Come to think of it, my landlord told me after the fact that Brent approached him about purchasing the building that my lounge is in. Do you think he could've been interested in taking over your building?"

He dipped the SG meter into the sample. "It's likely. The guy was exorbitantly wealthy, and he made a big show about it when he was here. He mentioned that he had investments in other distilleries. If he had such a problem with the way I do things here, it'd make more sense for him to put me out of business rather than invest a dime or acquire it." He jotted down the SG reading in the notebook.

"What brought Brent here, of all places?"

Logan shook his head. "No clue, man. But I guess he was looking to expand his empire. Hope Mills draws a lot of tourism, and I'll bet he saw an opportunity to make a buck. We might never know the truth, though."

Between its colonial history, proximity to nature, unique artisan shops, and thriving culinary industry, Hope Mills was a popular getaway from the hustle and bustle of Philadelphia. Thanks to a burgeoning arts and theater scene, our town was a cultural destination, so I wasn't surprised Brent might have been looking to invest in it.

If Logan had figured out Brent was looking to buy his space from his landlord, he'd have the same apparent motive as Heidi or me, in the eyes of the investigators, to kill Brent. Unlike me, though, Logan was aware of his wealth and business prospecting before his death.

He wandered to another fermentation tank, and I lingered behind him. "But regardless of his potential business dealings, what he wrote on my business card makes me look terrible. What if the police believe I killed him to avoid repayment? I didn't owe him a cent."

"Is there anyone you *do* owe money to?"

Logan blinked hard. "Nah. I mean I have a small business loan, but I'm all caught up on my payments and pay all my rent and other expenses on time every month. My credit is immaculate."

So he does lease.

A muffled pounding sound thwacked faintly from the front of the distillery.

I cupped a hand around my ear. "Do you hear that?"

"Huh, that's strange." He raised an index finger toward me so we could listen more closely.

The banging continued through the ambient drone of the distilling equipment around us.

"Come on." He waved for me to follow him, and I did.

As soon as he opened the metal door which led to the tasting room, my stomach dropped the second I saw Cam and Detective Sharp peering into the distillery's glass front door.

Logan unlocked it, allowing the two of them to step inside.

Detective Sharp and Cam each placed hands on their hips and stood with their feet planted confidently shoulder-width apart.

I wiped an imaginary bead of sweat from my forehead, hoping they wouldn't suspect I was interfering. I prepared to justify my visit, grateful I had placed an order which Logan had entered into his system.

"Good afternoon, Mr. Parker," Detective Sharp nodded.

I greeted her in return.

Logan stepped forward. "How can I help you two?"

"Mr. Nelson," Detective Sharp's booming voice echoed through the tasting room, "we need to speak with you ... alone." Her eyes drifted to me.

Taking the hint, I gave a small wave and made my way out the front door.

As soon as the door clicked shut behind me, I sidestepped, keeping my back against the building's brick exterior.

Luckily, I could still make out a faint trace of the voices inside.

I could've sworn I overheard the detective say, "What do you know about the false alarm triggered at D'Amico's last night?"

TWENTY

Not wanting the police or Logan to catch me loitering, I fled the distillery, rushing away from the building's large front windows and past the police vehicles parked outside.

According to my watch, DCDC was set to open about fifteen minutes later, and my heart sunk for Logan. I knew firsthand how bad the investigation could make his business look to the community. It was the reason I felt so desperate to find answers.

On the other hand, a tinge of anger forced its way into my mind. Could Logan have had something to do with the false alarm from the night before? And considering Kristin's bracelet which was left behind, did he know something about her disappearance? I hated the thoughts running through my head, but I couldn't resist wondering if I'd been alone with Brent's killer. If Brent had been looking to buy him out, or if Logan had debts he wasn't confessing to, he could've had motive.

The image of Kristin's bracelet wouldn't leave my mind as I headed back to my car in the sputtering rain, both hands tucked firmly in my pockets. Though she'd been reported missing, I'd seen her the prior morning while she was supposedly unreachable.

Finding Kristin had to be a key to the case.

Considering her involvement with the Lifted Spirits and rapport with Will, I figured he must be concerned about Kristin if he knew she was missing. Maybe Will knew something which might clue me in to her whereabouts. However, I feared I might have been the last person to see her as she sped out of Brent's driveway.

I drove down Main Street, away from the downtown area.

Similar to my landlord's realty office, Will's financial advising business was in a large, butter-yellow Victorian home with a spacious wraparound porch, stained-glass windows, and beautiful landscaping lining the sidewalk leading up to its front steps. The sign above the door read KAUFMAN AND ROTH FINANCIAL PLANNING.

Many small businesses in downtown Hope Mills—like small law practices, therapists, realtors, and doctors—had offices in similar historic houses, which been rezoned and converted for commercial use. I loved how our quaint town had preserved the historic homes, keeping the town's homey feel alive.

I inched into a parking space on the street outside of Will's office as I remembered it was Saturday. Would he even be there? It was possible he had weekend office hours, but I wasn't counting on it.

I stared at the yellow building from my car, questioning if it was even worth my time to try to chat with Will.

When I spotted movement in one of the old home's bay windows along its front porch, I froze. Will paced behind the window with both arms behind his back as he gazed outside.

He locked eyes with me and waved to gesture me to come inside. I'd have no choice but to explain myself for lurking.

Inside the house, I turned left in the main hallway to enter Will's office. He was already standing in the center of the spacious room with high, ornate ceilings, ready to greet me. He wore a slate-gray sportscoat over a powder blue shirt and dark-wash jeans. There were dark circles under his eyes. "I wasn't expecting to see you here today, Reece. Are you ready to take me up on that offer to help you manage some assets?"

As concerned as I was about ensuring Subplot's profitability, I was diligent enough to manage my own financials without paying for an advisor. However, it was a great way to hopefully get Will talking. "I've given it some thought," I white-lied. "I wasn't sure if you worked on Saturdays."

"I'm here pretty much every day, whether I'm seeing clients or not. Even Sundays." He gestured toward a leather armchair in front of his ornate, polished desk, which looked to be made from a dark walnut or cherry wood. "Please, come in. Take a seat." Beneath the bay window behind him was a golden cart with a few partially-filled whiskey decanters and upside-down rocks glasses. "Can I pour you something?"

I waved my hands in front of my chest as I leaned back in the chair. "I'm crafting some new drinks for our summer menu this afternoon, so I'll get my fix later."

"What can I help you with?" He placed both hands behind his head and reclined in his ergonomic desk chair.

"I hope I'm not wasting your time here, but I'm not here to chat about business."

He lowered his hands and straightened his posture. "Oh? Is it something about what happened the other night?"

I pressed my lips together. "I'm sure you've heard that Kristin has gone missing." I was careful not to mention spotting her outside of Brent's house or discovering her bracelet under the fire alarm at D'Amico's the night before.

He sighed. "I have. I've been worried sick." He pointed

toward his eyes. "You can probably tell I've barely slept. I, along with some of her friends and family, were out canvassing the town last night. We posted some signs and searched high and low, talking to anyone we could that might have seen her somewhere."

"I saw a bunch of signs throughout town this morning."

Will's tired eyes stared into his desk's glossy, varnished wood. "I have a feeling she didn't just disappear on her own volition. I'm worried someone's trying to harm her."

"But who? Do you think it was Brent's killer? Maybe she saw something after the meeting she shouldn't have, and they've kidnapped her to silence her."

"It's possible, but I have a different theory." He rose from his chair and closed the drapes, dimming the room, which was only lit by a lamp on his desk and another in a corner behind me. Outside of his office door, he turned on a white noise machine, presumably to drown out our conversation, before closing the door and taking his seat again.

"Brent was a very important man. Are you familiar with Crestmore Enterprises?"

"Vaguely. I think I've seen it on a sign in a storefront here in town." I didn't want to appear like I knew as much as I did.

"Brent was a real estate mogul and developer. As you know, Hope Mills brings in some out-of-towners, and he was trying to swoop in and buy up a bunch of property. Crestmore Enterprises owns a variety of brands, and he was trying to bring them into town."

I was glad Will could validate the other information I'd gathered about Brent. But what did it have to do with Kristin?

"And Kristin, as you might be aware, is on our borough council. She's been very vocal at council meetings about not letting multi-million dollar developers, such as Crestmore Enterprises, into Hope Mills."

"But if his company wanted to buy up property in town, isn't that their prerogative?"

"Well, sort of."

I scratched at the stubble under my chin. "The council can't stop someone from buying property, though."

He tapped his fingertips together one by one. "True. But Kristin was working to propose laws that would've restricted chain businesses from coming to town, made zoning ordinances stricter, and denied building permits for such endeavors. Kristin was doing a lot to make Brent's life difficult. And honestly, rightfully so. I don't want our town to be taken over by corporate overlords. I imagine a new business owner like you would feel the same, too."

I nodded in agreement.

Will sat stiff in his chair. "Call me crazy, but I think someone from his company—maybe one of his business partners—could be holding her hostage as payback for all the roadblocks she caused. And if they suspect she could've been responsible for his death? In that case, I have no doubt they're the reason no one can get ahold of her. The day after he died—and shortly before she went missing—she told me someone from the Crestmore organization dug up ... a video ... from her past."

"What kind of video?" I braced myself.

"An adult video. They threatened to resurface it."

I about choked on my own breath. "That's downright evil. Why would they do such a thing?"

He folded his hands on his desk and stared down at them. "I don't believe it's anything to be ashamed of, but she doesn't want to be connected to the video anymore, especially now that she's dipping her toe in politics. The video had been made with her consent, although that was fifteen years ago, and it was still circulating, as much as she tried to bury it. Because they threatened to connect her to the video, which would ruin her political aspirations, I don't think she had much choice but to do their bidding."

My lips tensed into an angry pucker. "That's absolutely awful and inhumane. Nobody deserves to be treated that way. Please tell me you've shared this with the police."

"Absolutely. But I guess when the leader of such a prominent organization ends up dead, someone has to pay the price. I'm not going to let some multi-millionaire maniacs get away with such despicable actions, all in the name of making even more money—and that's coming from a guy whose job is to help people build wealth."

Will's xylophone ringtone blasted from his phone on what seemed like the maximum volume, causing him to jerk in his seat. "Oh, my. I need to take this. Personal business. You can stay there."

He darted out of the room. As soon as the door latched behind him, I scanned the office to see if there was anything else I might glean from my visit.

Due to the white noise machine playing just outside the door, I couldn't make out even the slightest muffle from Will's phone conversation. I needed to act fast because I'd have no clue when Will would be coming back into the room.

I sprung to my feet and hustled behind the desk.

On Will's computer screen was what looked like a financial software with numbers and line graphs in one window. Just behind it was another window with a checklist for managing assets for deceased clients with a few items checked off— contact estate attorney, notify beneficiaries, freeze accounts.

Though the checklist could've been for any client, I couldn't help but wonder if Brent was a client of Will's. Had Will placated Brent at the Lifted Spirits meeting because he didn't want to lose such a wealthy, prestigious client's business?

Will's desk was organized with only a few papers and envelopes on it. The first was an unopened piece of mail addressed to Will with no return address, but with NOTICE OF DEBT FORGIVENESS in bold capital letters printed across the top of the envelope.

Careful not to touch anything, I squinted at the document beneath it, which appeared to be a medical bill from a nearby university hospital. Unfortunately, important details were covered, so I couldn't tell who it was addressed to.

Beside it was a letter to Will from an auto lender that his account was in delinquent status.

I stood up straight as I put the pieces together. *Is Will in financial trouble?* I had a difficult time reconciling that Will was a financial advisor, yet he appeared to be struggling himself, although it wasn't my place to pass judgment.

I hurried around to the front of the desk, but the door clicked open before I could take my seat.

Busted.

"Is everything alright?" I asked, as if it wasn't unusual that I was standing several steps away from where I'd been sitting when Will left the room.

He let out a heavy sigh as the door latched shut behind him. "As good as it can be. It's been a rough time."

Since he was being vague, I figured it was best not to pry.

If Will had turned on the white noise machine to drown out our conversation about Kristin and Brent's murder, then I doubted he would've taken a call on the subject in the hallway.

I took a seat in the chair I shouldn't have left. "Back to what we were talking about, were you in touch with Kristin often before all of this happened?"

He sat behind his desk, glancing at the papers on his desk as he did. "I was. She's the treasurer of Lifted Spirits, so we were in touch fairly often, and she's usually quick to respond."

I was surprised the club was big enough to have a treasurer, but it seemed like the Lifted Spirits members took the club pretty seriously.

"When she stopped answering my calls and texts, I swung by her house. There was no answer, and her car was gone. I've driven by a few other times, and it was the same."

I wondered if she drove the silver car I'd spotted her driving outside of Brent's house, though I doubted it, given how easy it was to track license plates.

Luckily, he didn't make any comment on why I'd been standing when he came back into the room. I prayed he didn't suspect I'd been snooping. I'd only wanted to see if he might have other details related to Brent or Kristin that he hadn't shared with me, not discover private information about him.

"So, what do we do?" I asked.

He folded his hands on his desk, and his tired eyes fixated on them. "At this stage, I'm not sure there's much else we can do. I've told the police all I know, so it's in their hands now. I don't want to give up hope, but I'm starting to feel defeated."

I wasn't so close to giving up.

TWENTY-ONE

I was deep in focus as I lifted a large tray of sizzling candied bacon from the oven. After my conversations with Chloe, Logan, and Will that morning, I needed to do something with my hands to keep my mind from spiraling.

"Good afternoon," Ava's voice rang out, causing me to lurch in surprise. I hadn't heard her footsteps approaching or any doors opening. As far as I was aware, I'd been alone in Subplot.

Luckily, I hadn't dropped the baking sheet filled with sputtering hot bacon grease as I quickly spun around to see Ava standing in the kitchen doorframe dressed in her usual all-black attire.

I panted as I slid the tray onto the stovetop with an oven mitt-clad hand. "You scared me, A." I couldn't help but chuckle when it sunk in I wasn't in any real danger, but it didn't stop me from pressing both hands firmly on my chest in relief.

She stepped into the tight kitchen space. "Sorry. I didn't mean to scare you." She grimaced. "My bad."

"No, no. It's alright." My rapid heart rate decelerated to its typical rhythm. "I'm on high alert with everything going on, ya know?"

She stepped further into our small kitchen and wafted the sweet, smoky scent toward her nostrils. "Also, we need to make a candle that smells exactly like this kitchen. This might be the best thing I've smelled in all my life, and I need to taste whatever this bacon creation is ASAP."

"I attempted to make candied bacon." I stepped aside and opened the refrigerator, revealing several cooling trays of the sweet-and-savory treats.

"Based on the smell of it, I'd say you succeeded."

"I needed something to keep me busy this afternoon, so I decided it was a good day to test out our snack menu. And by menu, I mean this bacon and a small batch of hummus we can serve with pita and vegetables."

To prepare it, I'd laid out strips of thick-cut raw bacon over a wire rack and foil-lined baking sheet to catch the drippings. Then, I brushed on a mixture of DCDC double-barrel bourbon, brown sugar, black pepper, and the slightest hint of chili powder for a subtle kick before baking it.

Ava and I briefly discussed the portion size and pricing for our new menu addition before she headed to the bar to start prepping ingredients for the evening's service.

Since Subplot first opened, we'd mainly used our kitchen to prep elements for our beverages. We made all our syrups in-house rather than buying ingredients made with additives or from a wholesaler. Additionally, we pressed our own juices and blended our own fruit purees whenever possible to deliver the freshest, highest quality drinks.

Eventually, I hoped to launch a full menu of small bites so customers could nosh on candied bacon, marinated olives, charcuterie trays, or enjoy a seasonal dessert special as they sipped their drinks. I also planned to partner with local businesses to feature their food on our small menu—such as baked goods from Jackie and Jill's, the local bakery, or gelato from D'Amico's.

After cutting each slice of bacon into thirds and stacking them in a large tub in layers between parchment paper, I designed bookmark-sized flyers on my laptop in the office to promote our new snack offerings. I printed off a stack on cream-colored cardstock, grabbed a pair of scissors, and joined Ava at the bar.

As I carefully cut each sheet of paper into six bookmarks we'd insert into our hardcover book menus, Ava sliced limes into wedges.

"You'll never guess what happened earlier today."

Ava paused from cutting her lime to glance down at me. "Hm?"

I kept my eyes focused on cutting the bookmarks as straight as I could. "I was near DCDC, and I knew we were running low on bourbon, so I swung by to place an order with Logan in person. While I was there, the police officer and detective showed up. They wanted to speak with him to see what he knew about the false alarm." I hoped sharing the tidbit about Logan might help me open up a dialogue about what was going on between them.

Ava rested her knife on the cutting board. "They think he pulled it?"

"I'm not sure, but I wonder if it's a possibility. The cops asked me to leave before they got into any specifics with him, and I only overheard a quick mention of the false alarm."

Ava took off her vinyl gloves. Her eyes were wide and unblinking. "If they think he pulled the alarm, he could be in big trouble."

I studied her face as she moved her lips ever so slightly. Was she rehearsing what she'd say next? Was she trying to keep her story straight? Was she trying to make sense of what she knew about Logan?

Her eyes glazed over. "No, no, no," she whispered to herself. She shook her head as if she was in denial. "Why would he have done that?"

I leaned forward, ready to put a comforting hand on her shoulder. "Are you alright?" I felt bad for raising the subject after seeing how much it upset her.

Tears welled in her eyes. "And there goes my mascara."

"You can talk to me." I solemnly patted the bar. "There's been some weird and scary stuff happening around here this week, and my priority is making sure you're safe. Is there something going on with Logan? You don't have to protect him."

"You can't tell anyone."

"I won't. But I need to know you're okay."

"And especially not the cops. If it turns out he did pull the alarm, you absolutely cannot repeat what I'm about to share."

Although I didn't want to make any promises, I couldn't pass up learning more details. "Ava, you have my word."

"Logan and I are together."

"You are?" My jaw hung open. After years of working with Ava and a couple of months doing business with Logan, I didn't have any inclination they might be dating. During the time they'd both been in my sphere, I hadn't seen them interact much. Considering Ava's eagerness to help him unload whenever he made a delivery, I should've guessed. Perhaps I'd been too wrapped up in my own personal situation to notice.

Ava surveyed the lounge as if making sure no one else could hear her revelation, although we weren't yet open to the public. "I've been trying to keep it under wraps."

I lowered my voice to a whisper to appease Ava. "Why is it such a secret? Do you think he had something to do with

Brent's death?" I asked, although it seemed unlikely Ava would incriminate her secret boyfriend.

"What? No." She shook her head and let out a small chuckle. "No," she repeated, spoken more firmly and with a stern facial expression the second time. "It has nothing to do with that. It's—"

"So, were you two arguing that night after all?" I tried asking again, even though she'd denied it the night before.

She sighed. "He's been wanting to go public with our relationship, and I've been hesitant. We had a chat about it while we strolled around after leaving the meeting. We weren't arguing. He was frustrated, that's all. He's a great guy. I'm just not ready for anyone to know about ... us ... quite yet."

I rolled my shoulders and stretched casually, hoping she wouldn't perceive me as a threat. "Is there any particular reason you don't feel ready to go public with your relationship?"

Her facial features went slack and shoulders drooped. "Mixology is such a male-dominated space. I'm trying to make a name for myself as a mixologist, and I'm interested in getting into distilling. But with Logan being so respected in the industry, I guess I'm insecure. I don't want it to seem like I'm riding his coattails or getting a free ride because of our relationship."

"I'd never think that in a million years." I slid the stack of bookmark flyers to the side in front of me. "You have one of the best palates of anyone I know, and your innovation with flavor is next-level. You take risks behind the bar, and it always pays off—big time. You'd make a name for yourself in this industry with or without Logan. You're extremely talented."

Ava tightened her lips and nodded at me, acknowledging my words. I hoped she believed I was sincere. "*You* might believe that. It's the rest of the industry and the world I'm worried about.

Unfortunately, I understood her fears. Although more

women than men were bartenders in the United States, it didn't make being a woman in mixology any easier. Customers often stereotyped women in the field.

For example, men at the bar sometimes questioned Ava's knowledge about certain spirits or how to craft various cocktails. They subscribed to the ridiculous and unfounded belief that the craft and appreciation of liquor was a man's game.

Even worse was when they tried to mansplain facts or classic cocktail recipes to her.

Plus, when I attended my first mixology conference to learn from some of the greatest mixologists in the business, I was shocked to find nearly every session was led by a man. Only one woman had a speaking session during the entire weekend-long event—and she presented on the challenges of being a woman in the industry. It didn't make sense to me how over half of professional mixologists were women, yet they were underrepresented—or ignored completely—when it came to being treated as experts.

It was a heartbreaking realization for me, and I felt committed to doing whatever I could to promote equity in our field.

"Are you happy with him? Career concerns aside, he better treat you well." I scratched at a bump in the bar's varnish.

Ava put both hands over her face before sliding them down the sides of her neck. "That's what makes this so hard. He's such a great guy, but I'm worried what other people will think. I want to be judged on my own talent, not who I'm dating."

I rubbed my hands together. "But you'd have a passion for spirits and mixology regardless of Logan. And if a mutual passion brings you two closer, it's all the more beautiful."

She sighed. "You're right, but I ..." She paused. "Please don't tell anyone we're together."

"It's safe with me."

"Especially now. If Logan actually did pull the fire alarm ..." She folded her arms and grunted. "If he did it, we're done. What was he *thinking*? I'm going to look really bad if word gets out about us. People around town are going to think *I* had something to do with this murder."

Why did Ava keep speaking as if Logan could've pulled the alarm? She'd just claimed he was a great guy, but she also wasn't giving him much benefit of the doubt.

Was she aware of his potential motive? If she knew Brent was interested in potentially buying out DCDC, could she have been an accomplice to Logan? Could she have poisoned Brent somehow during the Lifted Spirits tasting, as a twisted sign of love and devotion? She'd been handling the snifter glasses that night, and Logan had been pouring, so either of them could've slipped him something when no one was looking.

I scratched at my beard. "Is there anything Logan did or said recently that would make you believe he had reason to pull the alarm?"

She flinched. "We don't even know for sure if he did pull the alarm." Her flash of defensiveness made me question whether she knew more than she let on. "He hasn't said anything unusual or out of the ordinary."

"I'm only asking because I care. If Logan had darker motivations, you could be in danger. Has he been acting strange lately?"

Before I finished asking my question, she shook her head adamantly. "No. Not that I could tell." She caressed a hand over her chin, and glanced up at the ceiling as if she was reconsidering. "Although, he did tell me the police found his business card in Brent's pocket and he was being questioned about it. The only reason I can think of for him to pull the fire alarm would be to try and steer the police in a different direction, but I think it's pretty far-fetched, don't you?"

"And risky," I added. "Plus, based on how the detective talked last night—and the fact they followed up on it this morning—it seems like the police are connecting that incident with the murder."

Ava let out a groan and paced back and forth behind the bar. "He couldn't have done it. If he thought it would distract the police, it clearly backfired."

"On a related subject ..." The words slipped out of my mouth with no filter. "Did you really find Brent's wallet in the restroom the other night?"

Ava froze in her tracks and stared at me as if she was in disbelief from the far end of the bar. "Huh?"

"Did you really find it, or did it find its way into the lounge another way?"

"Why? You think I had something to do with it? Or Logan?"

"He was in the lounge not long before you found the wallet. Were you covering for him?"

She folded her arms again. "You're pointing a lot of fingers today, Reece. If you're trying to clear yourself of suspicion, go talk to someone else."

Ouch.

I immediately regretted asking Ava about the wallet.

Despite feeling guilty about my misstep, I couldn't help but be wary of her stark shifts in demeanor. Was she cracking under the pressure of my questions? Though she was hesitant to go public about her relationship with Logan, could she have been lethally devoted to him?

What were those two up to?

Could Logan and Ava have acted together? If they did, could their relationship have been a front for two partners in crime?

TWENTY-TWO

About twenty minutes before six, subdued electronic house music floated through Subplot. On Saturday nights, we hired Tessa, a local DJ who went by the stage name DJ Leo Moon when she performed.

Shortly after her soft, yet energizing ambient beats began swelling through the lounge, Lainey climbed the stairs to unlock the secret bookcase entrance and begin welcoming the first groups of the evening. The music was more akin to something one might listen to while studying or at an upscale rooftop lounge than anything that might play at a nightclub or wedding reception. It brought a relaxed mood into our intimate space.

Dante turned off the fluorescent lights, plunging the lounge into its cozy amber glow and further establishing the chill ambiance DJ Leo Moon's music created.

A couple of minutes later, Lainey's voice rang through my earpiece. "Reece, if you have a moment, could you come upstairs? Heidi wants to speak to you."

What now? We're opening in three minutes. This better be good.

Dante smirked from across the lounge. "Oooh, someone's in trouble."

I ran my tongue along the inside of my lower lip as I stifled a grin. "I'll be up in a sec," I answered into the tiny lapel mic clipped on my shirt.

Ava stayed silent and didn't look up as she arranged bar tools at her station, further cementing my guilt for letting my suspicions get the best of me during our earlier conversation.

When I opened the secret bookcase, I didn't have a chance to confer with Lainey, who smiled timidly as Heidi leaned on her hostess stand with a hand on one hip.

"Everyone sitting at my bar is all lined up for you." Heidi turned around and gestured to the restaurant behind her, visible through floor-to-ceiling windows in our common entryway.

Usually, customers trickled into Subplot during the first hour or two we were open, but it seemed like we'd have a full house from the get-go.

"Wow, that's great. I'm glad to see they're giving you business while they wait to come downstairs."

Heidi rolled her eyes. "Do you mind funneling them upstairs to grab some dinner after you liquor them up?"

"Do you have a spare stack of menus?" I hoped appeasing Heidi would keep me in her good graces and maybe earn me some new information if she'd heard new gossip floating around her restaurant. "I can keep a few downstairs to hand out when customers ask if we have a food menu." I didn't mention we were testing out a small bites menu for the first time, featuring our bourbon candied bacon and hummus with pita chips and vegetables. However, customers always asked about food, and if they needed more than a snack, it'd be convenient to have D'Amico's menus available as a talking point to send them upstairs.

Her face lit up in a way I'd never seen. "You'd do that?" she asked in a whispery voice.

"Of course. That's what neighbors are for." I flashed her my widest grin.

"Can you come to my office? I'll grab the menus."

Without answering, I turned to Lainey and gave her a shrug before following Heidi through the double glass doors which led into the restaurant. As we stepped inside, my nostrils were delighted by savory scents of tomato and cream sauces and toasty garlic bread.

"Now for the real reason I called you up here." She used her eyes and a subtle jerk of the head to gesture toward the bar. "I'm sure you've heard about the councilwoman they're searching town for."

"Isn't it terrible?"

She flipped a lock of her wavy brunette hair over her shoulder. "I'm not so convinced she's actually missing. Anyway, her friend is here. She was with him before the tasting the other night."

My gaze shifted across the restaurant. I immediately recognized Theo's curly brown hair. Squinting to take a closer look, he appeared jovial, laughing with a group of friends at the bar.

"Keep an eye on him, would you?" Did Heidi view me as an ally now? "I find it a bit odd that he's out having a great time while his friend is missing. Besides the murder, it's the talk of the town, so there's no way he isn't aware. Maybe he's here to try and scope things out or plant evidence."

Could Theo's apparent lack of concern signal that Kristin wasn't in any real danger? To Heidi's point, the town was plastered with signs seeking tips on her whereabouts, so he had to be aware.

To our left, Heidi pushed a solid wood door which led to her cluttered, tiny office. "Now, let me get you those menus."

The door must've been weighted because it slammed shut behind us as soon as we stepped inside. I couldn't tell if the uneasy tightness in my throat was paranoia or my self-protection instincts kicking in.

She rifled through stacks of paper. It was a wonder she could find anything in there.

"Ah! Here we go." She grasped a thick pile of glossy takeout brochures and waved them at me. "Here, take these. No need to return them. Your customers can take them if they like. I can have more printed up." Her pearly white teeth beamed at me in a way I didn't know was possible.

I grinned in return as I grabbed the menus. While I was in her good graces, I figured it was my best shot at asking a few questions based on some of the details I'd gathered about the case.

"Has the detective asked you any questions about a receipt?"

"Receipt?"

She had to know what I was talking about, right?

"I heard a receipt from D'Amico's was found in Brent's pocket after he was murdered, along with one of Logan's business cards from the distillery." I hoped sharing the tidbit about Logan might encourage her to open up and keep her from feeling like I was singling her out.

The color drained from her face. She fanned out her fingers and inspected her nails rather than making eye contact with me. "How did you know about that?"

Know. "Oh, you know how rumors spread. Plus, one of the whiskey club members told me it looked like Brent had been overserved at your bar before their tasting on Wednesday. I thought the receipt would help your case since you said you didn't serve him any alcohol."

She gasped, but still didn't look me in the eye. "I'll bet the loudmouth from borough council told you that. Don't believe a word that came out of her mouth. Like I said before, I don't think she's actually missing. I think she killed him."

I rested my chin between my thumb and index finger. "Kristin Marshall? You're not concerned something terrible might've happened to her, too? The search efforts around town seem pretty serious."

Heidi tsked. "It's all lies. I'm sure she was trying to throw me under the bus, all so she could avoid being charged with Brent's murder. It had to have been her. I think she's guilty and the authorities can't get in touch with her, so of course they want to track her down."

I released the tension building in my clenched jaw. "In any case, when we spoke about this a few days ago, you were confident Brent wasn't served a drop of alcohol here."

She rolled her eyes. "The receipt they found shows he was only rung up for one drink."

Heidi did know about the receipt, after all.

"Even if it was one drink, you lied. And your name was even listed on the receipt as the server."

What was she hiding?

In an instant, Heidi's demeanor switched from cold and defensive to overwhelmed. The color drained from her face and small beads of sweat formed near her hairline.

"I cracked under the pressure, okay?" She reached for the desk chair behind her. She fumbled through a drawer in her desk and grabbed a wad of brown paper napkins, using them to dab her forehead. "When you and I spoke, I didn't realize he'd kept the receipt, let alone consider it'd be evidence in this case."

"When the police came to talk to you, did you tell them the truth about serving him?"

"Of course I did. I needed to explain my little spat with Brent was over his check and nothing more."

"What else would they have thought it was about?"

She crumpled the dampened napkin in one hand. "Kristin told them we were arguing about Brent trying to buy the building. D'Amico's is my family's legacy, but I wouldn't have killed a man for it."

"Wait. Did Mr. Percy tell you anything about Brent's interest in buying this building?"

"No! I didn't learn about that until the police questioned me. They'd heard it from Kristin. She was the one on borough council trying to keep Brent's empire from taking over Hope Mills. I applaud her work on that front, but if she thought I knew something about it, she was wrong." Heidi began to tear the thinning napkin into shreds with shaky fingers. "And why would Mr. Percy tell *me* such a thing?"

"You said you two are close. I figured he might've clued you in so that you had time to adjust—instead of just pulling the rug out from under you."

She tossed the scraps into a wastebasket under her desk. "We are close—but from a business perspective. If he was planning to sell the building, wouldn't you think he'd keep it to himself until the deal was signed and laugh his merry way to the bank?"

Was she bluffing? I'd already caught her in a lie. Was her dispute about drinks with Brent actually an argument about potentially losing her business?

While I appreciated her perspective, I wanted her to answer my earlier question. "So, it was just one drink?"

She lifted a hand up to her brow, shielding her eyes. "No. My bartender Tommy served Brent three drinks."

"Three?"

She fidgeted with the collar of her blouse. "When Tommy handed him his receipt, he argued over the cost of his meal and asked to speak with a manager. For someone who was supposedly very wealthy, he made a big stink about prices."

"So that's when you got involved?"

Her breath hitched as she inhaled. "I voided Tommy's transactions, and rung Brent up for one drink. He was being such a pain. I should've comped his check and been done with it, but I wanted to get whatever money I could and send him on his way. But even three drinks is hardly overserving."

That explained why Heidi's name was listed as the server on the receipt. Depending on what he drank and how much time he spent at the bar, I agreed with her. However, the quantity was a still a discrepancy.

Based on everything Heidi shared, Kristin's original recollection of events was true, although I couldn't know for sure what she and Brent argued about.

Kristin had told the truth about Brent being served several drinks at D'Amico's prior to the Lifted Spirits meeting, which helped her credibility. On the other hand, Heidi had lied to escape suspicion.

I was starting to consider Will's theory that someone from Crestmore Enterprises might be holding her under duress with her video as collateral. And if she was responsible for pulling the fire alarm the night before, could they have put her up to the task as a form of revenge?

If only Kristin hadn't gone missing. It seemed like she had all the answers I was looking for.

If there was still a chance Heidi had something to do with Brent's death, could she know something about Kristin's whereabouts?

TWENTY-THREE

I peeked at my watch. 7:03. "Sorry, but I've got to run," I told Heidi before exiting her office. "It's time to open the lounge."

I stepped into the vestibule and gave Lainey the thumbs-up to begin texting customers who'd put their names on the wait list.

"Alrighty!" she responded in her typical, bubbly way. "You better get a few deep breaths in now, because I don't think you'll have a chance to later. The wait list is already stacked."

"Bring it on!" I pumped a fist at my side.

She sent text messages to our first batch of customers via our mobile app, and within thirty seconds, the first group of four reported to the secret bookcase.

It was Theo's group.

"This place is awesome. Wait till you see how much thought they put into every detail," he proclaimed to his friends.

Considering Kristin was allegedly missing, he appeared to be in good spirits. Perhaps they weren't friends outside of the whiskey club, but I still found it odd. Had he come to the lounge for fun? Or was he scoping things out? He hadn't been on my personal suspect list, but I couldn't be too cautious with anyone, especially considering his proximity to Kristin and the fact that he'd been in the lounge that night.

"You're back!" I gave him two thumbs up, trying to appear friendly as I welcomed him. "I recognize you from a few nights back."

Theo grimaced. "Yeah, I don't think I'll be going to another of those meetings." He glanced uncomfortably around his circle of friends. "You guys head down without me. I'm going to catch up with Reece for a second."

I turned to Lainey, who gave me an acknowledging nod before leading Theo's friends downstairs.

"You won't be going back to another Lifted Spirits meeting?" I asked as the secret bookcase latched shut.

"I mean ..." He took a deep breath and lowered his voice. "You saw how it ended the other night. And now Kristin's missing."

I let out a quick, audible exhale. "Did you hear anything from her after the meeting?"

"Nah. We're friends within the club, and we'll grab a bite to eat together before meetings from time to time, but we didn't spend much time together outside of that."

He paused while a couple entered the vestibule and opened the glass doors to D'Amico's dining room.

"Do you have any idea where she could have gone? Did she say anything?"

He shrugged and shook his head. "Sorry, but I don't know anything else beyond what you and I both witnessed on Wednesday night."

Between his upbeat demeanor and casual attitude regarding Kristin's disappearance, I had an inkling he knew more than he let on. Perhaps he had reason to believe Kristin wasn't in danger.

"Well, even if I don't catch you at another Lifted Spirits meeting, I'm glad to see you back at Subplot."

"What I will say is ... the club is bad news, man."

"How so?"

"I don't know. They take it so seriously. I'm not trying to get mixed up in any drama. Good vibes only for me, and that group is anything *but* good vibes."

His response felt like a non-answer. I got the sense that he knew more about the Lifted Spirits than he was willing to share.

The bookcase entrance unlatched, and Lainey returned to her podium. My time alone with Theo was up, but I hoped I could learn more about the whiskey club. Maybe that was my key to learning more about Kristin's disappearance and Brent's death.

"I'll take you downstairs," I told him.

He took a seat with his friends, and I joined Ava behind the bar. Although tensions were high between us, we managed to put our conflict aside as soon as Subplot opened. I was grateful we respected each other enough as professionals to put our cocktails and customers first, despite the pressures from the investigation.

As the night went on, we maintained strong communication as we navigated around each other at the bar with ease. We worked together like one efficient machine.

"Uh-oh. We're running low on limes," I mentioned as I crafted a twist on a daiquiri at a customer's request. "I'll have to prep some more before we run out."

Ava tightened the lid on a cocktail shaker. "Don't worry. There's another tub prepped in the kitchen fridge. I sliced some extras tonight. I had a feeling we'd be especially busy." She began shaking the cocktail.

"Thanks, A." The loud ice clinking in her metal shaker

drowned out my words, but I continued talking anyway. "You're always one step ahead of me."

She must've heard me because she grinned in return.

For the most part, our Saturday evening was routine. I kept anticipating another catastrophe to happen after three consecutive nights of misfortune.

What could possibly go wrong tonight? The question replayed in my head as the evening went on.

That was until a few minutes later when Lainey seated a group of six in leather reading chairs around a bean-shaped coffee table in my section. The group consisted of three women and three men, one of whom stole my attention immediately.

From the second I laid my eyes on him, butterflies erupted in my stomach. The back of my neck felt like Ava had set it on fire with the blowtorch we used to smoke cocktails.

As he took his seat, I admired the way his wavy brown hair bounced. I reveled in the smirk he directed at one of his friends, fantasizing it was meant for me.

He was the worker I'd spotted a couple of days before at Ampersand, the new bookstore in town.

He wore a royal-blue woven button-down shirt over white linen pants that hugged him in all the right places. Tan penny loafers with exposed ankles and a silver necklace completed his sophisticated look.

My mouth grew dry.

My knees grew shaky.

What I wouldn't have given to wait on any table but his. I would've preferred to wait on Cam and Detective Sharp.

Regardless of how attractive I found the bookseller, I wasn't ready to talk to him, still feeling emotionally raw after my conversation with Chloe earlier in the day.

My heart pounded harder and faster with every step closer to the group.

"Good evening, everyone. My name is Reece, and I'm one of the mixologists here at Subplot," I said. "Have any of you been here before?"

They all shook their heads.

"Great. Well then, welcome, everyone." I clapped my hands and rubbed them together nervously. I pointed at the stack of books on the coffee table at their knees. "The books in front of you are your menus. I'll grab you some water while you read it over, and we'll go from there. Let me know if you have any questions."

"Are you the owner of this place?" my crush asked from the far side of the circle of friends.

Two of his friends and about six feet separated us, but the shivers surging down my spine were as though he'd caressed me, brushing my neck with his soft breath.

Why was he asking if I owned the lounge? Was something wrong? Did he not like it? Was my zipper down? Amid all my internal questions, I cocked my head and answered hesitantly. "Yes, I am."

His rich brown eyes traced the neon light strips around the upper perimeter of the lounge. "If the cocktails are as amazing as the atmosphere, we'll have to come back every week." He traced the inside of his lower lip with his tongue, oozing with charisma and making me swoon inside.

Yes, please do, I thought, quickly followed by, *Actually, please don't. I don't think I could handle the stress.*

"Yeah, this space is sick," one of his friends chimed in.

"The vibe down here is so chill. The music adds such a cool ambience," another friend added before taking a panning video from one side of the lounge to the other, presumably to post to social media.

Once she finished recording her video clip, I let out an embarrassed giggle. "I hope the quality of the cocktails *exceed* the atmosphere." I clapped my hands together again. "I'll be right back with some waters."

I sped behind the bar as if I was floating.

Ava sprinkled espresso powder on an espresso martini, using a paper coaster to keep the garnish in a straight line. "Are you crushing on one of the girls at that table?" She carefully placed three coffee beans on the other half of the drink, which hadn't been dusted with the powder.

"At which table?"

She threw her head back and let out a boisterous laugh. "Don't play coy with me. The table you practically skipped over here from fifteen seconds ago."

I jerked my head back and furrowed my brow. "No. Why would you think that?" I chuckled.

If only she knew. Though I'd known Ava for many years and spent more of my waking hours with her than anyone else, I still hadn't come out to her. I rarely spoke about my personal life at work. For example, she knew Chloe and I had broken up, but I hadn't shared the reasons why. I certainly hadn't told her I was gay yet. Until I told my parents, I couldn't bring myself to tell other people in my life.

She turned her head down but stared up at me with her eyes as a smirk grew on her face. "You're usually as cool as a cucumber. I watched you wait on that table. You acted so nervous." She slid the cocktails she'd finished to the end of the bar, ready for Dante to pick up and deliver to one of his tables.

"No, I'm not crushing on anyone. They were giving me lots of kudos on the lounge, and I got shy. I should be more graceful about accepting compliments."

Ava giggled and shook her head at me. "I know how proud you are of this space. *That* wasn't how you usually respond to compliments." She picked up the next order ticket off the bar.

"But it's none of my business." There was an excited lightness in her voice.

She has me figured out.

Thankfully, Ava's frustration from earlier seemed to have melted away.

"Hey, maybe you know something about me I don't even know myself," I joked as I filled six short glasses with water, although it was more likely I was terrible at disguising my true feelings. I crouched down to grab a carafe of cold water from the fridge behind the bar.

When I stood back up, I was surprised she still stood in front of me. "Reece, I'm sorry for losing my temper earlier. I'm sure you know as well as anyone the stress from this week is ... a lot. I should've trusted you have my best interest at heart."

I tightened my lips and nodded as a melancholy wave washed over me. Before I could respond, she was already scooping ice into a cocktail shaker.

"And I apologize for pushing the subject so hard. If you're in any danger or have any concerns, I hope you know you can come to me if you ever need anything."

I returned to my crush's group with water and took each person's order. He ordered the Green Gables cocktail.

He liked tequila and matcha? Two of my favorite things in the world.

Eventually, Theo and his friends finished their drinks and paid for their tab. He waved at me from across the lounge on his way out. I reflected on our earlier conversation, realizing it left me with more questions than answers.

Did he have intel on Will or Kristin? Had he known Brent better than he let on? Or was he sleuthing around himself? It was entirely possible he'd come to Subplot to observe me or Ava. Was he secretly on the lookout for Kristin? Could he somehow have been involved in her disappearance?

Later in the evening when my crush's group was about ready to leave, I brought their check sandwiched in a worn mass market paperback of *The Da Vinci Code*.

He extended his arm in my direction. "I've got this one," he told his friends.

"Seriously, Julian?" one of the women in the circle scolded.

Julian. Julian. Julian.

The name repeated through my mind.

Julian and Reece? Or Reece and Julian? Reece and Julian totally sounds better. I rolled my shoulders to expel the thought.

"I can pay for my own drinks," one of the guys offered.

"Are you alright?" another woman in the group asked.

Realizing she was looking at me, and when no one else answered her, I placed a hand over my chest. "Who, me?"

All eyes were on me. The entire group bobbed their heads up and down, nearly in perfect unison.

"Oh, I had a quick shiver, that's all." If the bead of sweat forming on my brow was visible, it was probably obvious how nervous I was.

Maybe Ava was right. I wasn't as good at hiding my nerves as I thought.

Julian quickly placed his credit card in the paperback with a cracked spine and handed it to me with a twinkle in his eye before any of his friends could intercept.

I deepened my voice and bowed my head. "Thank you."

Thankfully, when I returned behind the bar to close out the group's tab, Ava waited on a table Lainey had recently seated in her section, so she wasn't there to tease my obvious uneasiness.

After swiping his card, I read the name Julian Garcia over and over as I placed it back into the book with a pen clipped over the cover while I waited for the receipt to print.

Over the next ten minutes, I returned Julian's credit card

and receipt, the group wrapped up their conversation and left, and I cleaned up their seating area.

When I opened the mass market paperback to retrieve the final signed receipt, I wasn't only delighted by a generous thirty percent tip—Julian also jotted his phone number below his signature.

Am I dreaming?

Thank goodness Ava, Lainey, and Dante hadn't seen this.

I stuffed the receipt into my pocket and scanned the lounge to make sure neither of them had watched me.

As exhilarating as it was to have my crush's phone number —especially knowing *he* took the initiative to make a move— my heart plunged as I considered how far from ready I was to move forward. I was in no position to be dating.

If he's interested in me at all.

Perhaps he just wanted to be friends or learn more about Subplot.

But a number written on a receipt seemed flirtatious. I'd seen customers use that move before.

Not only was I still grieving the end of my relationship— which I'd caused—but I also had a long coming out journey ahead of me if I wanted to even *consider* dating. I didn't feel like it was fair to a potential partner if I hadn't yet come out to all my loved ones. Julian's bold move gave me the sense he was much farther along on his journey than I was. I'd never even kissed a guy, let alone pursued dating one.

As badly as I wanted to text him right away, I snapped the book shut, swallowed my shame, and accepted that I didn't know when—or if—I'd be ready to make the next move.

TWENTY-FOUR

At the end of the night, Ava flipped on the overhead industrial lights. Tessa, a.k.a. DJ Leo Moon, packed up her equipment, and I helped by carrying each large speaker out to her van parked in the back alley. I sent her payment via my mobile banking app and confirmed she received it.

"See you next week?" I asked.

Tessa hopped into the driver's seat of her van. "Same time, same place." She pulled her door shut and drove away.

Although it would've been nice to make more small talk, I didn't want to linger for too long in the alley behind the lounge. Plus, at two a.m., I was sure she wanted to go to sleep as much as I did.

I headed inside to close out our bookkeeping in the office. After running a sales report for the evening, the revenue our new snack offerings had generated both shocked and delighted me. The hummus and candied bacon I'd concocted out of stress turned out to be a huge success.

At least something was working in my favor.

To make sure I could believe the evening's revenue break-down, I checked the fridge to make sure we'd sold as much as the report showed. Taking note of the empty tubs sitting on a countertop in the kitchen, I felt a joyous sense of pride knowing we'd sold out. Our small bites would be here to stay.

Ava unloaded clean glasses from the dishwasher and placed them back on their shelves. After she finished, Dante loaded it with the remaining used glasses he'd collected from the lounge along with our bar utensils. He and Lainey each grabbed a spray bottle and worked their way around the lounge, wiping down tables, picking up stray trash, straightening chairs, and fluffing pillows.

I carried a large green push broom from the supply closet into the main lounge. "Thank you all for your hard work tonight, everyone. I don't think we've been that busy since opening weekend, and it couldn't have run any smoother. I can take it from here. Why don't you all go home and get some rest?"

Lainey glanced up as she straightened a stack of books on a coffee table. "Are you sure?"

Dante continued wiping down a table. "I don't mind staying to help."

I nodded. "Does anyone need a ride home tonight? I want you all to be safe."

Lainey slid the pile of books to the table's center. "My boyfriend's picking me up."

Ava organized bar tools at her mixology station. "I drove here today. I'm not walking alone at this hour until all the madness in town is over."

"Are you parked nearby?" I asked.

She pointed upward. "On the street right outside of D'Amico's."

I looked to Dante. "And you?"

"Same as Ava."

I breathed a sigh of relief. "Good. I'm glad you all have a safe way home. Please send me a text when you make it back. There's no such thing as being too careful considering the circumstances."

Lainey and Dante headed upstairs first. Ava stayed a few minutes longer to wipe down the few remaining tables before collecting her purse from the office and leaving the lounge. "Goodnight, Reece." She waved three fingers while her hand grasped a lanyard loaded with keys, a hot-pink keychain bottle opener, and a pocket-sized can of pepper spray.

"You're sure you don't want me to walk you to your car?"

Ava shook her head gently. "I'll be fine. See you tomorrow."

After her light footsteps pattered up the stairs and the secret bookcase opened and closed, Natalie Imbruglia's "Torn" kicked off my shuffled playlist of songs by women of the nineties. I resumed sweeping and taking care of other closing tasks around the lounge, including straightening up spirits and supplies behind the bar and gathering the evening's trash.

Before stepping into the alley to throw a large black bag of trash in the dumpster, I stood facing the glowing red exit sign which hung above the back door.

It's going to be okay. It's just to the dumpster and back.

I tightened my grip around the garbage bag as sweat formed in my palms, which caused the plastic to slip.

I pressed the door's exit bar and pushed my way out to the alley, which was dimly lit by an orange-tinted light affixed to the side of the building.

I paced down the alley to the dumpster. *You're alright. You're fine.*

I was haunted by a flashback of Brent's body on the ground —his flannel-clad arm vivid in my mind—as I stepped carefully, keeping my eyes on my feet and trying to keep my breathing steady.

Once I reached the dumpster, I flung the bag of trash into it and immediately turned back to the lounge's door.

That wasn't so bad, was it? I took a deep breath.

After taking my first steps back toward Subplot, one of the bushes lining the alley rustled as I approached it. I gasped and diverted my path back to the lounge to stay as far away from the bush as possible.

Could it have been the wind? Or maybe a squirrel?

The rustling intensified. It was definitely *not* the wind.

When the noise repeated, only one bush moved.

I knew something bad was going to happen tonight.

I patted every pocket of my jeans. My phone must've been in the office.

I jogged down the alley until I reached the lounge's door and glanced over my shoulder to make sure I wasn't being followed. My hand gripped the cold metal handle, and I stayed completely still to listen for any other movement.

"Meoooow." The high-pitched sound was long and drawn-out.

Was that an actual cat, or was someone tricking me?

I released my grip from the door handle and stepped cautiously toward the bush.

"Meoooow." The sound was too shrill, yet faint to have been made by a human. Was someone trying to lure me into the bushes by playing a cat's mew on a speaker?

I took another tiptoe closer to the bush, and it rustled again.

I jerked backwards.

The silhouette of a tiny cat jumped out of the bush and sidled cautiously toward me in the dim light. "Meooooow."

I squinted, helping me see an orange tabby cat with a patch of white fur streaked across its face.

"Hey, little ... fella?" I spoke to the cat in a falsetto tone. "You're just a kitten, aren't you?"

It took a few small steps closer to me, and before I knew it, I had a kitten butting its head into my calf. It rubbed the full length of its body along my leg. I crouched down, and as my ears got closer, I could hear the tiny kitten purring.

I couldn't resist extending my hand, and the cat eagerly sniffed my fingers before butting its head into them, coaxing me to pet and scratch him.

Maybe it was the sadness from my breakup, the vulnerability I felt in light of the investigation, or my exhaustion at two in the morning after a long work day, but I fell in love immediately.

I scratched behind its ears, and it plopped down on the gravel, clearly relishing every second of affection I could give. "I can't leave you out here," I said in my sing-songy talking-to-animals voice.

Although I'd had dogs and cats as family pets throughout my childhood, I never had a pet as an adult. With Chloe and I working in the bar and restaurant industry for our entire adulthood, we both tended to work long, irregular, and often unpredictable hours. And when we weren't working, we were on the go, spending our weekends hiking, at art and music festivals, and going on trips, so it never made sense to have a furry companion, as much as we both wanted one.

The cat wasn't wearing a collar, so I had no way to know if it belonged to someone. Stray cats weren't very common in Hope Mills, so it was difficult to imagine the affectionate cat didn't already have a home.

Though I couldn't tell if the cat was a boy or girl, I instantly knew I wanted to name it Jameson after the Irish whiskey brand.

"Meoooooow." Although I didn't speak fluent feline, I got the sense Jameson was hungry from the urgency in his meow.

Given it was the middle of the night, all the animal shelters, pet stores, and grocery stores in the area were closed. I racked my brain thinking of possibilities to find food for Jameson. I could Google what human foods were safe for cats to eat. But then again, my fridges here and at home weren't well-stocked.

And then it dawned on me. Chloe's parents had a cat—a sassy calico named Maggie May, a nod to her mom's obsession with Rod Stewart. As much as it pained me to try calling Chloe, especially after spending my evening yearning for Julian, I felt confident she'd still be awake after the late Saturday shift at the bar where she worked. Plus, her big heart for animals would be the quickest and easiest solution to find food for Jameson until the animal shelter opened.

I scooped him up off the gravel alleyway, and he relaxed in my arm. He couldn't have been more than five pounds. Where I'd expected him to be skittish or resist being held, he nuzzled into me.

With my free hand, I pulled open the downstairs door to Subplot, locked it behind me, and carried Jameson to my office, closing the door so I wouldn't lose him somewhere in the lounge.

I placed him on the floor and sat in my desk chair before reaching for my phone on the desk. Based on his calmness and how quickly he'd socialized with me, I didn't believe he was feral.

As I listened to the dial tone ringing in my ear, hoping Chloe would answer, Jameson jumped up onto my lap and laid down.

"Reece, is everything okay? What's wrong?" Chloe spoke quickly and with concern.

Considering the time, she likely thought I was in trouble, perhaps tied up in something related to the investigation.

"Hey, Chlo. I'm fine. Everything's okay, and I'm sorry for the late call." I cleared my throat. "I know it's super late, but I figured you'd still be up."

"Yeah, I just finished closing the bar, and I'm driving home now. What's up? This doesn't have anything to do with the case, does it?"

"No."

She let out a relieved sigh.

"When I took out the trash tonight, I found a kitten in the alley behind my lounge. I think he's hungry. Could I borrow some of Maggie May's food for him? I'm happy to pay for it."

"Meooooow." Jameson let out another long, urgent plea for food.

"Oh my goodness, was that the cat?" Chloe crooned through the phone. "Bless its *wittle heawt*," she squeaked in her talking-to-animals voice.

"Yep, it was. I'm calling him Jameson."

"I'll be home in the next ten minutes. Do you want to swing by my parent's house? I can grab some food for him."

"That'd be great." As Jameson purred and stretched in my lap, I observed his matted, dirty fur. He'd likely endured the loud thunder and pouring rain outside earlier. My heart broke as I considered how scared he must've been. "I'll meet you there soon. Thank you so much for taking my call and helping me out. I'm sure I caught you off guard."

"I got you."

When I pulled up to Chloe's parents' house, Jameson was curled up in my lap, purring. Chloe leaned against her red SUV in the driveway, waiting for me to arrive.

I lifted him off my legs and placed him in the passenger seat. Although I didn't think he'd run away from me, the last thing I wanted was for Jameson to flee while I figured out a way to get him food.

"Where is he?" Chloe asked eagerly.

I waved her over to follow me to the passenger-side door. "He's right there." I pointed inside.

Chloe leaned forward and peered into the window. "Aww!" Her voice curved upward as she laid eyes on the kitten. She placed both hands over her chest and stuck out her lower lip— the same look she used to give me when she really wanted me to do something but didn't think I'd be on board. I was a sucker for that look. "I'll run in the house and bring you a bag of food. I'll be right back."

While I waited for Chloe to return, I leaned against the side of my car and studied the vibrant night sky. The clouds from earlier in the day had rolled through, and the skies were clear and speckled with stars. Chloe's rural street was void of street-lights, so I was lit only by the moon and starlight shining above.

A few minutes later, the screen door opened and slammed shut. Chloe returned with a gallon-sized bag filled with dry cat food.

"Thanks so much, Chlo. I can give you some cash for this and return whatever is left over."

She closed her eyes and shook her head. "Don't worry about it. I'm happy to help a kitty. But wait here another minute. I have more things to give you."

After going back inside the house for another couple of minutes, she returned with a small bag of kitty litter and a litter pan with a scoop.

"You had these laying around?"

"My parents occasionally foster kittens, so they had extra supplies in the garage. You came to the right place."

"Are you sure I can't pay you for all of this stuff?"

"Positive. You can donate whatever's left to the shelter. I'm sure they'll be happy with any food they can get, even if it's a small bag like that one."

"Thanks, babe." The words slipped out of my mouth. My chest tightened. I didn't intend to send mixed signals. "Sorry, I ..." I stuttered. "Thanks a million."

"You're welcome." She tightened her lips and rocked on her heels.

"Well, it's late, and we should both get some sleep." I squinted down at the dark pavement at my feet before pacing around my car to get in on the driver's side. "Thanks again."

We said our goodbyes, and I squatted into my car. I scooped a small handful of food out of the plastic bag with my hand and dumped the small portion in front of Jameson on the seat, who began to scarf down the dry food as I pulled out of the driveway.

For so long, my world felt like it was crumbling around me, but caring for Jameson made me feel like at least one thing was working out like it was supposed to.

TWENTY-FIVE

I awoke the next morning to the rhythmic vibration of Jameson's purring on my chest as he nuzzled his head into my jawline.

As I opened my eyes, he meowed as if he was asking a question.

"Good morning, buddy." I slid my arms from under the covers as gently as I could, not wanting to scare him away by moving too quickly. I scratched behind his ears, and his eyes closed as if I'd pushed him over the line into bliss.

After gathering supplies from Chloe the night before, I'd set up a bowl of dry food and water in the kitchen with a litter pan nearby. Not long after, I'd quickly drifted off to sleep, and upon waking found it was ten-thirty—not bad for being awake until almost four.

As I walked into the kitchen, I noticed Jameson not only made a dent in his food, but he'd also used the litter box. The night before, I'd been so tired I hadn't considered whether he was litter trained. It was a relief to see Jameson was housebroken, which gave me faith his owner was somewhere nearby.

I snapped a photo of the handsome kitten on my phone and

posted it to every Hope Mills community page on social media I could find. In my post, I mentioned where I'd found him, provided a physical description, stated he was safe and sound, and included my phone number so his owner could get hold of me.

I created a simple flyer on my laptop and printed a stack of forty-three sheets I planned to disseminate at the Hope Mills Farmers' Market. I'd intended to print more, but my printer ran out of ink after forty-three.

"Be good while I'm gone," I told Jameson as I locked my front door from the inside, one arm holding the stack of flyers against my ribs. Though I was slightly anxious about what trouble he might get into while I was away, there wasn't a ton he could get into or destroy. My apartment was practically empty, so there wasn't much damage he could do. "I'll be back in a little bit."

Jameson's eyes gleamed, and I couldn't help but sense sadness in them. My heart broke as I considered I'd be leaving him alone again. My main source of comfort was the prospect of helping him find his way back home.

I slipped out the door and put on my sunglasses. The sun beamed warmly on my arms and neck, and the humidity in the air made the upper-sixties morning feel warmer than it truly was.

Multi-colored canopies lined the Promenade where, each Sunday, local vendors sold fresh fruits and vegetables, hand-made jewelry, vintage clothing, woodwork, and more. I admired the bustling crowd. It seemed like the whole commu-nity—and likely visitors, too—came out to support the vendors each week, so I felt confident it would be a good opportunity to search for Jameson's owner.

I started by chatting with an artisanal candlemaker, who happily displayed the flyer to get the word out about Jameson.

As I meandered from tent to tent, I overheard snippets of conversation which highlighted the town's curiosity surrounding Brent's murder.

"The guy was from Kentucky. I hear they're sending his body back there for a memorial service," a customer told the woman selling hot sauce under a red canopy. "It really is a shame. No one deserves to go that way."

Two uniformed police officers stood along the Promenade, backs facing the river as they watched over the crowd. It wasn't typical for them to monitor the Sunday market, so I wondered if they were looking for clues or if their presence was to help community members and visitors feel safe.

I continued distributing flyers to each vendor. At one stand was a collective of Bucks County indie authors who banded together to sell paperbacks and bookish merchandise. I spoke with the group of authors about potentially hosting a reading and book signing in Subplot, which sparked some excitement.

After ducking out of their tent, I spotted Logan under a blue-and-white striped canopy across the lawn which was adjacent to the Promenade.

This was my chance to see what the police's visit was all about yesterday. I needed to find out once and for all if he had something to do with the false alarm, the mysterious appearance of Kristin's bracelet, and the vandalism on my bathroom mirror, which took a good deal of nail polish remover and elbow grease to scrub out.

While he chatted with a customer, I inspected a rack of upcycled denim jeans I had no interest in buying. As soon as the customer departed with a bottle and a sage-green T-shirt, I stepped back into the sun and made a beeline toward him.

"Hey, Logan. I didn't realize you had a tent at this market. I come most weeks and never noticed your stand."

He planted his hands confidently on his waist. "I usually

don't, but the vendor who is usually in this spot—the empanada stand—couldn't make it this week, so I had an opportunity to substitute. As bummed as I am about no empanadas, I've been wanting to give this market a try."

"How's the morning been so far?"

"I wouldn't say busy, but it's been steady. I have a feeling folks are too haunted by their hangovers from last night to purchase liquor first thing on a Sunday morning." He chuckled. He pointed at the stack of flyers under my arm and tilted his head to the side. "What do you have there?"

"Oh, these?" I fanned out the stack in front of me. "I found a kitten last night behind my lounge, and I'm looking for his owner. Would you be willing to display one of these at your stand so we can help him find his way home?"

"Absolutely. And I'll hang it up in my store when the market's over." He took a flyer and set it on the table, using two bottles of gin as paperweights. "Also, I have to address the elephant in the room. I know it didn't look good when the police came to speak with me."

I shifted my weight to one leg. "What did they want to chat about?" I didn't want him to realize I lingered outside briefly to eavesdrop.

He let out a deep sigh. "The fire alarm that was triggered in your building."

"What?" I craned my neck toward him, pretending this was new information. "Do they think you had something to do with it?" Regardless, I admired him for initiating the topic. Plus, his story was lining up with what I'd overheard, which was a good sign for his credibility.

Logan removed his trucker hat and ran a hand through his thick, wavy hair. "I swear I didn't pull it. It's all a huge misunderstanding."

"Why'd they think you'd know something about it, then?"

Logan hooked his thumb over his shiny silver belt buckle. "They reviewed Heidi's camera footage. The quality was fuzzy and dark—very low quality. She must still be using the first digital security cameras to ever hit the market. That being said, someone wearing all black, in baggy pants and a hoodie with the hood up, snuck into the restaurant. There's no footage of the person pulling the alarm, but this person went in and out the front door of D'Amico's minutes apart."

"Around the time the false alarm went off?"

"Bingo. This person walked in minutes before the alarm was pulled and rushed out into the breezeway along with everyone else when they evacuated."

I peered over Logan's head as I pondered theories about who could've done it and why. "I know a lot of people dress in all black, but wouldn't someone wearing a hood into an Italian restaurant stand out?"

Logan sucked in a sharp breath. "I guess everyone was too caught up in the chaos of the fire alarm to notice."

"And you couldn't make out any details like their hair color or any facial features?"

"No. Like I said, the video quality was terrible, and this person's baggy clothing covered them up. All I could make out was a dark, shadowy figure."

"I guess no one saw them head down into my lounge after they left the restaurant, then."

He crossed his arms over his chest, raising one hand to stroke his chin. "How do you know someone went down there?" His rigid stance made me wonder if he was being defensive. Did he really not know, or was he pretending?

"Because the mirror in my bathroom was vandalized. After the fire department gave us clearance to go back inside, Heidi and I did a quick walkthrough of the building with the detective. It had to have happened while we were evacuated."

"Sheesh." He shook his head disapprovingly.

"And between all those people and all the staff at D'Amico's, no one thought this person with their hood up seemed out of place?"

He twisted a lock of his wavy blond hair with one finger. "I asked the same question. I guess it was a busy night, and this person managed to tailgate in with a group and headed straight for the restrooms."

It had been a whirlwind of a night. "What does that have to do with you, then? Why did you get pulled into questioning for it?"

"Oh, right," Logan cleared his throat. "They wanted to see if I could identify the person from the footage."

"Could you?"

"No. It was impossible. Like I said, Heidi's cameras are dated. The quality was terrible—very grainy. I could only make out general shapes, especially considering how dim it was in there. One thing's for sure, though."

I cocked my head to the side. "What?"

"Whoever pulled the alarm dropped—or should I say planted—another of my business cards on their way out." His eyebrows narrowed. "One of the cameras further back in the restaurant captured them as they stepped aside and dropped something behind an empty table."

I turned my head away from Logan, as if I could visualize a whiteboard in the sky with all the information I'd gathered about the case. "But when Heidi and I did a sweep of the building with the detective, we never found it. I guess we must've overlooked that detail or mistook it for a piece of trash."

Or was Logan fabricating this part of the story so I'd rule him out?

"One of Heidi's waiters found it when they cleaned up at the end of the night."

"But this still doesn't make sense to me. Why would the police think you'd have any insight? You can't control who takes or distributes your business card."

"This card had another note scribbled on it. It said, *FALSE CLAIMS.*"

I scratched at my jawline. "Let me get this straight. Two of your business cards have been associated with this case. One found in the victim's pocket, and one found in D'Amico's after the false alarm incident. One says you owe money, and one accuses you of making false claims?"

"Neither of those things are true, but that's what they say." He gave a disgusted laugh. "Someone's trying to frame me. It's the only possibility."

I stared at the Washington Playhouse theater over Logan's shoulder as I attempted to snap mental puzzle pieces together in my mind. "Logic would say Brent wrote the first message—*OWES MONEY*—on the business card since they found it in his pocket, right? And you watched him take a card on the day he died. Unless he grabbed two cards, scribbled a different note on each, and then handed one off, I'd agree that someone's trying to make you look suspicious."

He let out a deep sigh. "I hadn't thought of it that way, but you're right. I can't fathom a single reason why anyone would want me to be mixed up in all this, though. I didn't do anything."

Possibilities flashed through my mind. I tried to remember what happened in the moments leading up to the fire alarm sounding a couple of nights prior.

Whoever pulled the alarm and dropped the card in D'Amico's must've been desperate to evade suspicion. Could Heidi have coordinated it? Maybe she'd asked someone to pull the alarm and drop the card to shift the police's attention to another business owner who might have been at risk for losing their space, given her knowledge of Brent's plans. Perhaps she intentionally glazed over it while we inspected the building. But if it was part of her ploy, wouldn't she have pointed it out to the detective immediately? While it seemed feasible, my theory had some clear holes and couldn't explain how Kristin's raccoon bracelet ended up in the restaurant.

"Have you said anything recently that could've been misinterpreted as a false claim?" I hoped he realized I asked from a helpful, rather than accusatory, place.

He folded both arms over his bulky chest. His eyes searched and lips moved without a word, making me believe he genuinely considered my question. "No. Any time I consider it, the only false claim that keeps playing out in my mind was what Brent said about me—when he said he wouldn't be surprised if my bourbon made him go blind or even worse."

The memory from the Lifted Spirits meeting came flooding back, accompanied by a tightness in my chest. "*FALSE CLAIMS* might be a false claim in itself. If someone was trying to frame you, the message wouldn't need to be rooted in truth. It'd just need to be suspicious enough to distract the police." I raised a swift index finger as another possibility entered my mind. "What if Brent's note—*OWES MONEY*—meant he believed someone owed *you*, not that you owed him or anyone else?"

Logan released his tight grip on his T-shirt sleeves and moved a hand to his hip. "It's funny you should say that."

I squinted from behind my sunglasses. "Hm?"

"I've been thinking a lot about the Lifted Spirits group. I still haven't received payment from the club for the bottles I brought to their tasting the other night."

Will had told me Kristin was the club's treasurer, meaning she was likely responsible for making payments. Considering she was missing or in hiding, I wasn't surprised that the payment hadn't been made. I also considered that due to her role in the club, she was probably aware they'd be tasting Logan's whiskey on the night of the murder. Did she use that knowledge as an opportunity to frame him?

Logan exhaled loudly, allowing his lips to vibrate as he pushed the air out. "And come to think of it, they hired me to bring a pop-up bar to a holiday party at Will's office back in December. It was a massive party with tons of guests."

"You were able to fit an entire bar setup in Will's office?"

"Oh, yes. Not his office specifically, but that huge house it's in has a large parlor for entertaining, seminars, meetings, et cetera."

"I didn't realize you bartended on the side."

"Yeah, in addition to running the distillery, I also bartend at private events. I'm trying to get away from it, especially since the distillery is taking off. I don't need to rely so much on the extra income. But I still haven't been paid for that holiday party, so I guess I shouldn't be surprised they never paid me for the bottles used at the tasting."

"Why did you agree to it, then?"

"I figured the Lifted Spirits tasting would get my new double-barrel bourbon some exposure. I only had to provide a few bottles, and even if they failed to pay me again, I knew it could lead to future sales. Since the tasting, several of the club's members have stopped into the distillery to buy bottles."

"I know Kristin is missing, so I hate to ask, but—"

"*Allegedly* missing," Logan interrupted. "I'll bet she's behind all of this, and she's in hiding." His theory aligned with Heidi's.

"Do you think she used her role as Treasurer to pay herself first, so to speak? If you weren't paid, could she have stolen from the club?" I didn't want to speculate, uncertain about the circumstances in which she was missing, but I couldn't help but connect the whiskey club's non-payment to the *OWES MONEY* note inscribed on Logan's business card found in Brent's pocket.

Had Brent been aware of Lifted Spirits' small debt and attended the meeting to scope out what they were up to?

But why?

"I think so." Logan removed his trucker hat to wipe sweat away from his brow. "Either she was stealing, or Lifted Spirits is actually a front for something darker."

"Darker? Like what? Besides the altercation with Brent, their meeting seemed pretty innocent to me."

He shrugged. "But look how it ended. Even if the club members aren't aware, maybe its leaders are laundering money or committing fraud for their own personal gain."

To go from non-payment for a holiday party to money laundering felt like a big jump. "But if that's what's up, there has to be a reason for it."

"Who knows?" He planted one of the pointed toes of his cowboy boots in the grass behind him. "Maybe they're trying to make a quick buck. Maybe they were trying to take some sort of political action against Brent."

"Hmm ..." I wasn't convinced, but I gave Logan's theory credit since it aligned with Theo's warning that the Lifted Spirits club was bad news. Was Theo aware that the club was facilitating illegal activity? Was this the bush he'd been beating around the night before?

"All I'm saying is I don't think it's a coincidence that Brent died immediately following the meeting. He was on to them, so someone put an end to him."

TWENTY-SIX

After meandering through the rest of the farmers' market and speaking with nearly every vendor, I slunk down into an Adirondack chair shaded by an oak tree in the center of the lawn and checked my phone to see if anyone had reached out about Jameson.

Though my posts in social media groups had been reshared dozens of times and received many comments, no one claimed him as their own or provided any information as to who his owner could be. I also hadn't received any phone calls or text messages, so I hoped the flyers I handed out at the market might reach new eyes.

As I sat, I did a double-take as a group approached.

I waited on them last night.

I spotted Julian's wavy brunette hair as the gentle wind blew it back. As the group strode in my direction, I debated hiding, running away, or standing up to chat with them. Recognizing both friends who accompanied him from the night before, I figured I could speak generally to the group, but if they picked up on the awkwardness Ava had sniffed out, I could expect to make a fool of myself.

As Julian passed by, I sat up in my seat to say hello, but my vocal cords wouldn't produce a sound. He caught my gaze out of the corner of his eye and gave me a slow, slight grin. And then he continued walking past me.

I hated that, to him, I probably appeared uninterested. I hadn't texted the number he was brave enough to leave for me, and I bet it stung.

Did Julian think I was unfriendly? Was he embarrassed for taking a risk?

Stop it, Reece.

I shook my head as if it could erase my attraction and halt the what-ifs playing out in my mind.

But naturally, my brain came up with a laundry list of reasons not to approach Julian and his friends. *I need to come out to my parents first. And I can't come out to them because I'm afraid of how they might react. And I shouldn't date until the crime scene behind my lounge has been cleared.*

Nate's voice transported me back to the present moment. "Do I need to build a cat tower?"

I blinked hard.

And there he was standing in front of me, wearing his usual garb—an olive-green and navy-blue plaid flannel with the sleeves rolled up, gray Carhartt work pants, and brown work boots. He also wore a backward gray baseball cap, presumably to keep the bright sun off his bald scalp. It didn't matter if it was Sunday or Christmas or if he took the day off. Like a cartoon character, he wore the same thing every time you saw him. Had I gotten married the day before, Nate would've been the best man in my wedding, and I'm sure it would've been a fight to get him in a suit.

"Is everyone in Hope Mills at the market today?" I pushed myself up from the Adirondack to stand beside Nate. "I swear

I've bumped into so many people I know already, and now here you are. I take it you saw the flyers I'm handing out?"

"Yup. And all your posts in the community groups online. No one's claiming the little guy?"

I sighed. "Nope. No one's gotten in touch with me yet."

"So, it sounds like you're keeping him." He spoke matter-of-factly, as if it was already a done deal. "I'll get to work on building that cat tower."

"No," I interjected more forcefully than I intended. "Sorry," I added with a chuckle. "I don't think it'd be right to keep him with everything going on in my life right now. And besides, I'm sure the little guy's owner must be around somewhere. Maybe he belongs to someone who isn't on social media or able to venture out of the house to the farmers' market."

"Don't you think you could use a little companion?"

"I mean, it'd be nice. But I don't want to put a cat-shaped bandage over this gaping hole I feel inside. It wouldn't be fair."

Nate folded his arms across his chest. "It sounds like the cat needs a home. I don't think he's concerned with what you think is fair."

The concept of home was important to Nate. We met in the eighth grade when he was a new student in our school. He came from a military family, so he moved around a lot until his dad was discharged and they permanently settled in Hope Mills. Because he'd done enough moving before the age of fourteen, he decided Hope Mills would be his forever home as soon as they settled in.

"And besides, I work a lot and have wacky hours. Shouldn't the cat be in a home where someone's around more?"

"But cats are independent. You wouldn't need to be around twenty-four-seven. Having a cat could be really good for you."

I tilted my head from side to side. "I'll think about it."

"Any new developments with what we were scoping out the other day?"

I puffed out my cheeks when I sighed. "It's been frustrating. After we did our little drive-by, I learned that the woman we saw driving the car down Brent's driveway had supposedly disappeared. That night, someone pulled a false fire alarm in D'Amico's and vandalized the mirror in my restroom. Her bracelet was found near the fire alarm in the restaurant. It all has to be connected to the murder somehow. There are several people who could've done it or may have been involved, and evidence connected to two of them were found in the building. The more I learn, the more questions I have."

Nate shook his head slowly. "On the bright side, it sounds like the police aren't as focused on you."

"True. But all this other stuff happening around me is really starting to take a toll. I want it all to end. Regardless of clearing Subplot's name from association, I want to figure out who did this so I can go back to running my business like normal."

"It's probably not much comfort, but at least you're not the only one this is happening to."

"What do you mean?"

"It seems like other businesses in town are being targeted, too. For one, if the false alarm was pulled in D'Amico's, could someone be targeting Heidi?"

My mouth went dry. "Heidi? She's a suspect, too. I think she knew Mr. Percy was entertaining an offer to sell our building, and I have proof she's lied about details related to the case."

He bowed his head and pinched the bridge of his nose. "I'm not sympathizing with her. I'm trying to show you the bigger picture."

I realized I was being unfair as I ranted to Nate, but I'd been too caught up in my emotions to admit it. Why do we show the worst of ourselves to the people we love and care about the most?

"And it's not just you and Heidi," he went on to say. "Someone vandalized Will's office last night or early this morning."

"Will Kaufman?"

Nate removed his ballcap and wiped the top of his forehead with the back of his forearm. "Yep—from Kaufman and Roth Financial Planning. Guess which local handyman got the call to make repairs?" He poked his thumb into his chest.

I harrumphed at the news. "Vandalism? As in spray-painted? What did it say?"

"No, there was no graffiti. Someone threw a rock through one of their front windows and smashed out the light fixtures on the front porch."

A chill crept up my spine as I pictured Will's financial planning office.

"Oh my goodness. I was just there yesterday. What is happening to this town?"

Why would someone vandalize Will's office? In my mind, the damage had to be related to Brent's murder. Destructive and disruptive acts were being committed against multiple people who'd interacted with Brent at the Lifted Spirits tasting hours before his death. My mirror and the missing wallet. Heidi's fire alarm. Kristin's disappearance. Will's office. Logan's inconveniently placed business cards.

My mind flashed back to the way Will pandered to Brent during the Lifted Spirits meeting. His diplomacy clearly rubbed Kristin the wrong way, and although it could be interpreted as suspicious, I wondered if the person who killed Brent was also after Will. Did he have to keep the peace with Brent to escape an untimely death of his own?

As much as I wanted to spend the afternoon hanging out

with Nate and forgetting about my responsibilities, I needed to help Jameson find his way home and uncover more answers about who was corrupting my formerly peaceful hometown.

"When are you going to head over there to start working on repairs?" I asked.

He glanced at his brown leather-banded watch. "Later this afternoon. Maybe in three, four hours."

"Before you go, I'd like to swing by and scope it out. Maybe I'll have an opportunity to chat with Will and see if he's learned anything more. Plus, it seems like the Lifted Spirits club is a front for something shady, so I want to see what I can uncover."

"Do you think he'll be in the office on a Sunday?"

"He told me he works pretty much every day. And who knows, he might be hanging around the office considering what happened there."

Nate crossed his arms over his burly chest. "Good point. But are you sure that's a good idea?"

"Oh, how the tables have turned. *You're* trying to talk *me* out of going?" I scratched my chin. "I'm curious to see if anything was left behind. Whoever's been causing this chaos has been dropping little clues, and I feel like I'm on the edge of discovering something big."

TWENTY-SEVEN

Before scoping out Will's office, I had one more important order of business to take care of—making sure Jameson could find his way home. By the time I returned to my apartment from the farmers' market in the early afternoon, I still hadn't received any messages in response to my search efforts.

Luckily, he hadn't destroyed my apartment while I was gone. I half-expected to return to find my leather couch clawed to shreds, but as far as I could tell, he hadn't gotten into any mischief. He'd made a dent in his food bowl, though.

His meow and soft purr approached before he nudged my shin, threading his small body between my legs and rubbing every square inch of himself he could against me.

I knelt to scratch him behind the ears and picked him up. Unlike other cats I'd interacted with, like Chloe's parents' Maggie May, he didn't resist being held in the slightest. Rather than squirming around, he relaxed into my arms and blinked slowly at me. In a documentary about cats I'd watched a couple of years prior, I learned that slow blinking was a feline's version of smiling.

I blinked slowly in return and scratched beneath his chin. I also discovered he loved to have his belly rubbed—a huge no-no for other cats.

I'd grown to be somewhat attached in the less than twenty-four hours since I'd found him, but I still felt a responsibility to reunite him with his rightful owner. What if a family was searching for him? He might have been a child's best friend or an older person's only companion.

While I waited for any signs from his owner, I decided to swing by the local animal shelter on the outskirts of town and check if anyone had gone searching for him there.

"Be still my heart!" the volunteer sitting at the front desk gasped, placing both hands over the chest of her lavender floral blouse. "Aren't you the cutest thing?" she asked in a baby voice. "And what's your name?"

I almost spoke in a high-pitched voice and waved Jameson's paw as if he was responding back to the volunteer but decided against it. "Unfortunately, I'm not sure of his true name, but I've been calling him Jameson. And my name is Reece." I waved and grinned, even though I wasn't in a smiling mood.

"And I'm Susan. It's a pleasure to meet you."

"I found this little guy in an alley yesterday, and I've been searching for his owner all morning." I raised Jameson higher when I spoke about him. "I've handed out flyers and made a ton of posts in different community groups online, but I haven't had any luck finding his owner. Has anyone come looking for him here?"

"Are you sure he's not a stray?"

Jameson nestled his head in the bend of my arm. He stared up at me with large, sad eyes which seemed to say, *You're not going to leave me here, are you?*

"I don't think he is. I took him into my home last night, and not only was he litter trained, but he also didn't destroy my apartment while I was away. He seems too well-trained and well-behaved—especially at his young age—to be a stray."

"Oh, I see." Susan folded her hands in a prayer-like way. "We haven't had any calls from anyone searching for a missing cat recently, but we can scan him for a microchip. If he has one, we should be able to pull up his owners' info right away."

She pulled out a black handheld device and waved it all around his tiny body. The scanner didn't make a sound. "Unfortunately, it doesn't seem like he has a chip, but if you'd be willing to foster Jameson, we can provide you with some donated food and supplies to ease your load. And then we can add him to our adoption listings to help him find a permanent home."

Even though I'd resisted Nate's persuasion to keep him, I felt committed to fostering Jameson until his owner was found. But considering we might never find his owner, the thought of listing him for someone else to adopt made me uneasy. On the flip side, I worried I might not make sense as his permanent owner given my schedule and lifestyle.

I clenched my eyes shut and pinched the bridge of my nose. "I'll foster Jameson, and we can add him to the adoption listings." Closing my eyes made the words vaguely bearable to say aloud.

Jameson shifted in my left arm, and the gentle vibration of his purr returned. When I opened my eyes, he gawked up at me attentively.

She clapped gently. "That's wonderful. It seems like you two have quite the connection already. I wouldn't be surprised if we have a *foster fail* on our hands."

I petted Jameson with my right hand, feeling a special bond with him but not yet ready to admit it out loud.

After completing a bunch of paperwork, Susan handed me a packet of information about fostering and caring for a cat. Next, she carried out a bin of donated supplies—a small bag of dry cat food, a few toys, a box of litter, and a scratch pad, which I hauled outside and loaded into the trunk of my car after placing Jameson in the front seat.

Taking Jameson in was another unplanned aspect of my life that felt like my world was spiraling out of control. Unlike breaking Chloe's heart, fearing coming out to my family and co-workers, and finding myself at the center of a homicide investigation, though, this was an unplanned event I was okay with.

After taking Jameson back to my apartment, the time approached two o'clock, and I texted Nate.

> Heading to Will's office now

> I'll let you know as soon as I'm done

A couple of minutes later, my phone dinged with a reply—a good reminder to put my phone on silent.

> Please be careful. Do you need backup?

> I should be fine.

I made sure Jameson had plenty of food, refreshed his water bowl, set up his new scratch board, and scattered his new toys around the living room before leaving for the next ten hours or so.

As soon as I was finished at Will's office, I'd need to head to Subplot to prepare for our Sunday evening service, which lasted from six to eleven—unlike our two a.m. close on Thursday through Saturday.

On my way to the Kaufman and Roth office, I strolled down

Main Street, which bustled with locals and tourists alike on beautiful weekend days.

Will's office, though still on Main Street, was further north of the busy downtown area, so I felt confident I could scope things out without drawing attention.

Once I reached the beautiful yellow Victorian, I immediately noticed the vandalism Nate had described. One of the front bay windows—on the other side of the porch from Will's office—had a jagged hole in the center with cracks snaking around it in every direction. The ornate porch light fixtures on either side of the front door were smashed, and even from the sidewalk, I could see broken glass scattered on the white-painted wooden porch below. Potted plants were knocked over, and their ceramic pots were either cracked or broken completely.

Standing where the walking path to the porch steps met the sidewalk, my feet felt glued to the cement.

Would Will be inside? If so, he might have details related to the vandalism which could be a missing piece in solving Brent's murder and Kristin's disappearance. If not, I planned to do a quick search for clues—no matter how small. Similar to how I'd found Kristin's bracelet near the fire alarm, I wondered if something else had been left behind.

However, knowing Nate had gotten the green light to clean up the glass and replace the broken light fixtures, I figured the police had already been by to survey the scene and collect their evidence. Regardless, I couldn't let this go until I scoped it out for myself.

Thwack. The muffled yet resonant thud sounded like it was coming from inside the house.

I spun on my heels toward the office, scanning the building from top to bottom, trying to locate where the sound came from, hoping it might repeat.

And then from Will's office, I saw the curtain move. Was he trying to get my attention? Was he in danger inside?

I prowled up the flower-lined walkway to the porch to get a clearer view. As I stepped closer to the house and into the shadow it cast, I could see a figure standing in the front window.

The figure appeared feminine.

It was Kristin.

Had she broken in? Was she searching for clues?

Help! She mouthed frantically in the window, waving her arms in fast yet controlled circles and not making a sound.

I gasped. Without much thought, I immediately headed toward the house's front steps with my eyes locked on hers.

She didn't blink. Terror was written on her face as her chin quivered. She placed a finger over her lips, and I turned my attention to my feet, careful not to make a sound.

Was Will holding her there? Or had someone put her up to breaking in? And how hadn't she caught anyone else's attention? Regardless, she was clearly in a terrible situation.

I needed to get inside the house—and fast—to save her.

I tiptoed up the front steps, avoiding the spilled soil from the overturned potted plants and shards of glass from the shattered window and light fixtures while still hurrying to her rescue.

As my fingers made contact with the golden door handle, I found myself wondering if it would even open. And if it did, how would I get to Kristin inside Will's office? Was she locked in there?

There's only one way to find out.

As I twisted the knob, the door unlatched. I cursed its creaking hinges as it swung open. Kristin had urged me to stay quiet, so I hoped the sound hadn't put either of us at any more risk.

Without closing the door behind me, I made an immediate left toward Will's office and grasped an intricate brass door-knob. To my surprise and relief, it twisted.

I gently pushed the door inward, revealing Kristin standing with feet shoulder-width apart—a pistol in hand and aimed straight at me. "Hands up." She spoke sternly and confidently, yet she trembled, as evidenced by the gun's barrel dancing in front of me.

I'd been so quick to run to her rescue that I hadn't considered it could've been a trap.

My breath hitched. I complied with her demand while following the moving gun with my eyes. "Whoa. I thought you needed help."

I fought against my instinct to pat my front pocket and try to discreetly slip out my phone. There was zero chance I could do it without her stopping me.

"I do need your help."

I cocked my head to one side and stammered, unable to say anything coherent. "How?"

"I need you to stay out of my way, even if I need to keep you out of my way for good."

"I take it you vandalized the porch?"

She nodded.

"How did you get in here?"

"How do you think?" Either her arms were getting tired or she was less focused on her aim, because the gun's barrel was no longer aimed directly at my face. "I let myself in."

"You mean you broke in?" My arms were also starting to go numb as I continued to hold them up. "But why?"

"When will you learn to keep your nose out of other people's business?"

"I'm guessing you're the one who pulled the fire alarm in

D'Amico's the other night? And vandalized the mirror in my restroom?"

The gun's barrel looped in a circular motion along with her eyeroll. "I tried to send you a warning sign to stay away, but you didn't listen. It's such a shame."

"But why?"

She readjusted the gun in her hand, once again pointing it directly at my face. "I saw you lurking outside Brent's house the other day. You were in a truck idling at the end of the driveway. You were with another guy. I knew you were on to me." Her finger flexed over the trigger but never came into contact with it. "And since you know the truth, you leave me no choice."

"But wait!" I panted as if I was out of breath, though I'd been frozen in place. "I don't think you killed Brent. Why would you have left your raccoon bracelet behind at D'Amico's? Wouldn't you have been more careful not to leave anything behind? I specifically commented on that bracelet when I ran into you at the coffee shop the day after Brent's murder."

Somehow, her eyes bulged even wider. Her shaking grew erratic.

"I think it was a cry for help. And you weren't at Subplot on the evening after the murder. So how did Brent's missing wallet make it into our restroom?"

"I—" she stuttered, putting the gun down at her side. Her chin and lips shuddered just as they had when she stood in the office window, luring me into the building. She shushed me with a pleading shimmer in her eyes.

"But Will was around that night. And why would you be hanging around a place you vandalized? It doesn't make any sense. Did he put you up to this? Did he talk you into vandalizing his office to make him look like a victim?"

"Why don't you ask him?" a man's voice asked from behind me.

TWENTY-EIGHT

I jolted, not realizing someone had followed me into the office. I spun around to see an almost unrecognizable Will hovering behind me.

His face was pale, and dark circles underscored his eyes. His usually clean-cut face was dotted with five o'clock shadow. Because he usually dressed to the nines with a tailored sports-coat at a minimum, his loose-fitting, tattered jeans and baggy hoodie made him appear severely underdressed and his lean frame appear wiry.

I lowered my arms and clutched my chest.

He advanced slowly on toward her, clapping his hands together slowly and unenthusiastically. "Wow, Kristin. Incredible. What a stellar performance." He turned his attention back to me. "Based on your reaction, I'd say she was a very convincing actress. Wouldn't you agree?"

I didn't say a word—only gave Will a death stare.

"If you thought she gave a good performance here, just wait until you see her leading role in a certain film that's about to hit the Internet." He pulled out his phone and wiggled his thumb over the illuminated screen.

Kristin's breathing turned shallow and erratic. "No. Please. Don't post it." She turned the gun toward Will, although her quivering would've made it impossible for her to fire an accurate shot. In her vulnerable state, I doubted she would even try to pull the trigger on him. "He made me do all this. He held me hostage, only letting me out of his sight to commit crimes to add confusion to the investigation. And the whole time he had his finger on the button."

"You're lucky I haven't posted it already. This bracelet you left behind is news to me. Sounds like someone didn't uphold her end of the bargain."

Brent and Crestmore Enterprises hadn't been blackmailing Kristin with her video—Will was.

"You're *disgusting*." I spat the words at Will. "You should be ashamed of yourself, but clearly you have no dignity."

He fished a pair of cotton gloves from the pocket of his navy-blue hoodie and put them on. He made a beckoning sign with an outstretched gloved hand. "Hand it over. Now."

As soon as Will took the gun from Kristin's hand, she crumpled, letting out a huge cry of relief, falling to the floor, and sobbing. *I'm so sorry,* she mouthed.

He dragged a finger along the weapon's barrel. "I had a feeling you'd swing by. You were lurking outside Brent's house the other day. Then you came here yesterday looking for clues. You just couldn't leave it alone. Now how do I make sure you don't blab to the police about this?" He gaped down at Kristin with wide eyes that didn't blink. "Don't worry, we'll still make it look like you killed him when it's all over."

"*You* killed Brent. It was you all along. You stole his wallet and planted it in my bathroom when you were at Subplot. You blackmailed Kristin into creating all the other chaos that's been happening around town."

He planted one foot in front of the other and raised the gun toward me. "Hands up." He didn't shake with the weapon in his hand like Kristin had.

I complied.

"There, isn't that better?" He spoke as if he was an elementary school teacher. His unblinking stare was intense, and his menacing demeanor indicated he wasn't in a rational frame of mind. "Now why would I do such a thing?"

I rolled my eyes.

"Go ahead. You've been sleuthing around all week looking for answers. Now's your chance to prove how right you were about everything."

"No."

He reaffirmed his stance with the gun. "I won't hesitate. We've already gotten this far."

I cleared my throat. "Brent was one of your clients, and I think you took advantage of him. You knew about his wealth, and I'm sure you knew about the business deals he was trying to make around Hope Mills to bring his empire here. He had enemies, and you saw an opportunity to position them as suspects in his murder. I think he was onto you, so you killed him to keep him quiet."

"Wow. Spot on. You deserve a gold star," he mocked.

I considered myself to be a peaceful man, but if Will hadn't been pointing a pistol at me, I would've struggled to keep my cool.

"Logan's business card was found in Brent's pocket after he died. The card had a note scribbled on it—*OWES MONEY*. At first, I thought Logan owed someone money, but I think his note meant *you* owed money to *Logan*. The Lifted Spirits club failed to pay him on multiple occasions."

Will chuckled. "Oh, boo-hoo. We owe Logan less than a grand. And besides, isn't it a treasurer's job to make payments?" His eyes fell to Kristin, who was still whimpering on the floor.

"Not when the club's president is in a financial crisis."

He tapped his foot. "I knew you were up to no good when you came to my office the other day. You were snooping, after all."

"I saw the medical bills and your debt mail. I wouldn't be shocked if you were stealing money from Lifted Spirits. You're a financial advisor. You understand how to move money around. And I'll bet when Kristin was going over the club's finances, she realized something was up, but you used your knowledge of her video so she'd do your dirty work."

Will's wrinkled eyebrows clenched, etching angry valleys all over his forehead.

My arms grew fatigued, still raised on either side of my head, but a sense of confidence washed over me as the pieces continued to click together. "And since I know you do, in fact, owe Logan money, I think Brent was onto you, too. You killed him to cover your tracks, didn't you? Why did you kill Brent?"

My straightforward question must've caught him off-guard. His wrists relaxed, and the gun no longer seemed to point between my eyes. His overall posture slumped, and his eyes drifted to the ground as they welled with tears.

Why the sudden shift? He appeared to be unstable.

His sadness was a stark contrast to his pointer finger, which still wiggled near the trigger. "I never meant for things to end up this way. My family was hit with hard times. My wife lost her job. And then she got sick. The medical bills kept piling up and our health insurance company denied some claims. Being a financial advisor, I knew how to move money around. It wasn't much. A little here, a little there. It wasn't right, and I'm not proud of it. But it happened. I only took from clients who had so much I didn't think they'd notice. I was going to make it right in the end."

In light of Will's plea, my breathing and heart rate slowed, and I felt a bit calmer despite the weapon in his hand.

"Will, it's not too late to turn things around." I softened my tone, trying my best to speak with compassion. "Could you please put the gun down? Imagine how much worse this could be for you if you don't. I'm sure we can come to some sort of agreement."

"No." He flexed the gun in his hands to reassert himself, and his posture tensed again. "I may work in finance, but it doesn't mean I'm rich by any means. I knew it was wrong to take advantage of my wealthy clients, but my family needed the money more than they did. I thought I could make it right before they even realized I'd moved their assets around. It was a small amount at first." As he spoke, his voice grew darker and more sinister. "But one lie led to another, and they kept growing a little bit bigger and a little bit bigger. Eventually, things got out of hand. I pilfered from the whiskey club's dues, which we planned to use to rent cabins in Tennessee for a group trip. When the funds came into question, I pinned it on Kristin, but she got defensive." He removed one hand from the gun to gesture toward her. "I had no choice but to dig up dirt on her so I'd have ammunition to keep her quiet. Her spicy material also came in handy to ensure she wouldn't tell the police about what I did to Brent. My dirty work did itself."

"And it ended in murder?"

"If anyone had it coming for them, it was Brent." Did Will think his sob story would make me sympathize with him? Did he think I might cover for him?

"Why do you say that?"

Will scoffed. "The guy was a jerk. You saw firsthand how he treated people. Plus, he was trying to buy up property all over Hope Mills. Any business that leased their space—including yours—was at risk of closing so he could bring in his own. His plan was going to ruin the soul of this town."

"But why would that justify killing him?"

"I'm telling you. My ... borrowing ... got out of hand. Brent was one of my clients. He was meticulous when it came to reviewing his accounts, and he realized I'd moved some money around I shouldn't have. He was a snake—digging around and interviewing my clients to learn more about me."

That explained why Brent had approached Logan and wrote OWES MONEY on his business card. He was doing research and keeping records of those Will had harmed financially.

"So, there." Any hint of sadness in Will's voice evaporated in an instant. "You have all the answers you've been searching for all week. And congratulations—the space you're leasing won't be bought out from underneath you. I did you a favor. Are you happy now? Now that you know everything, I have no choice but to get rid of you, too."

My breath hitched and became erratic. "No. Will. Please." My lower lip quivered uncontrollably as the rest of my body shivered in terror. I wanted to stay strong but being faced with my mortality made me beg by instinct.

My life flashed before my eyes as I watched Will's finger stroke the trigger, preparing for all my joy, regret, and hopes for the future to vanish in an instant.

A click echoed through the office, and before my mind could register what it was, I fell to the floor, hoping it hadn't been the sound of Will pulling the trigger.

TWENTY-NINE

"Freeze!" a man's deep voice ripped through the office, and heavy footsteps stormed through the hallway behind me.

Luckily, the unexpected invasion disoriented Will. While he still held the gun, his attention was focused on whoever had entered the room, and since I'd fallen, his aim likely would've missed me even if he had shot. I placed both hands on the back of my neck and rotated away from Will.

With his attention on the man who'd entered the room, I jerked my head toward the doorframe.

Cam aimed his gun at Will.

Detective Sharp followed closely behind. Her gun, pointed in the same direction, almost seemed to float as she crept carefully forward.

"Drop the gun *now!*" Cam's voice boomed. In all the time I'd known him, I'd never heard him raise his voice in such a way.

It was clearly effective. Will knelt down and placed the gun on the ground before raising both hands. He must've realized there was no way out of the situation without reaching his own bitter end. He turned his head toward the ornate wallpapered ceiling of his office as if to say, *I surrender.*

Detective Sharp remained in place as Cam approached Will. He unhooked a pair of handcuffs from his belt, and Will cooperated as he tightened them around his bony wrists. Cam told him he was under arrest and read him his Miranda Rights.

The detective approached Kristin, who hugged her knees and rocked back and forth as she sat on the floor, sobbing.

Thank goodness I left the front door open.

But how did they know I was in trouble?

While Cam and Detective Sharp dealt with Will and Kristin, Nate ran into the room. The sight of my best friend brought me instant relief. The tightness in my chest loosened, and I was finally able to take a deep breath.

"You two can go outside. But please don't go anywhere." Detective Sharp split eye contact between Nate and me. "We need to speak to these two privately."

Though I was shaky and weak, I pushed myself up off the ground and stood on both feet with the assistance of Nate's outstretched arm.

I followed him out to the front porch. Before sitting on a wooden swing that hung from the ceiling with metal chain links, he inspected it for loose shards of glass from the nearby broken window. "I'm so glad you're okay." His voice cracked as he spoke, and he put a comforting arm around my shoulder.

I embraced him in return, forcing a smile which felt impossible in my shocked state.

"How did ...?" I stammered. "I thought ... I ... I could be ... dead right now."

He removed his hand from my back. "When you told me you were scoping out the vandalism, I had a bad feeling. I decided to come over to make my repairs early in hopes I might catch you. When I got here, the front door was wide open, and I heard arguing inside. The whole thing seemed off, and I didn't want to take any chances, so I called the police right away."

I let out a heavy sigh. "Thank goodness you did."

He gulped hard. "I just wish I had stepped in to intervene myself, especially knowing now what kind of danger you were in."

"I'd say getting the police here as quick as you did was the most important thing you could've done."

"Thankfully, Cam must've been patrolling nearby when I called. He was here within a minute. The dispatcher must've alerted the detective, too, because she arrived just as Cam was running inside. I couldn't believe it all happened so fast, but I'm so glad it did."

As two vehicle engines roared down Main Street, I jerked in surprise.

They parked in front of the house with red, white, and blue lights flashing. Police officers I didn't recognize got out of each SUV and ran inside, barely acknowledging Nate and me.

A few minutes later, the two officers escorted Will and Kristin out of the building and down the front porch steps. He was in handcuffs, but she wasn't. The officer walking alongside a hunched-over Will held one of his arms and loaded him into the backseat of his vehicle. Kristin stared straight ahead as she walked freely beside the other officer, clearly shaken by all she'd been through. The officer held the back door of his SUV open for her, and she seemed to shiver as she climbed inside. Both police vehicles drove away, likely to transport Will and Kristin to the station for further questioning.

Cam and Detective Sharp stayed behind, each of them strolling out to join Nate and me on the porch.

Cam stepped forward, looking down at me on the swing. "What the hell was that?" A vein poked out of his temple. Though I could understand if his question came from a place of frustration, I knew it came from genuine concern. "You could've been killed. I thought we told you to stay far away from this investigation. And yet every suspect we spoke with mentioned how you came sleuthing around for information."

"I had to prove I had no association with Brent's murder. And besides, I interact with a lot of the suspects on a regular basis. What was I supposed to do? Not talk about the biggest news this town has seen in decades?"

"I was on your side this entire time. I know you. And I knew you couldn't have done something like this. But I had a job to do."

I broke off eye contact with Cam. Deep down, I felt silly for believing he doubted me—or worse, sought revenge. Despite what had happened between his sister and me, I should've trusted him to put justice first. "But the fact I found Brent. And where his body was found. The uncertainty of how exactly he might've been poisoned. Learning about his mission to buy up real estate and force out our town's small businesses. I felt like I needed to prove that despite those things, I wasn't involved whatsoever."

"So you involved yourself to prove you weren't involved?"

"Okay, you two. That's enough," Detective Sharp interrupted.

As raw as I felt, I realized Cam genuinely cared. He was the Cam I'd known all along—he was just trying to do his job.

"I'm going to need a summary of what exactly took place here between you, Ms. Marshall, and Mr. Kaufman this afternoon," Detective Sharp said. "I'd like you to come into the station to give your official statement."

I nodded.

Cam took a step forward. "I'll drive him to the station."

I caught a glimpse of the time on my watch. "It's almost time to prep the lounge. My staff will be arriving soon."

Nate gave me a quick pat on the back. "You should take the night off. Just focus on giving your statement and relax."

Taking the night off would've been in my best interest, although I couldn't imagine closing the lounge so last-minute.

"No, I need to work. I'll go after I leave the police station. It'll take my mind off things."

Cam shifted his weight from one leg to the other. "Are you sure that's a good idea?"

Nate removed his hand. "You were just held at gunpoint. You need some time to process your emotions."

Processing emotions. Maybe this was my chance to deal with what I've been through instead of distracting myself and avoiding my feelings.

Nate stood up in front of me. "Plus, you have a great team. I'm sure Ava, Lainey, and Dante could all manage at Subplot for one night without you. I can even pop into the lounge and fill them in."

I hoisted myself off the swing, my knees still trembling. "Could you? That'd be great. Please tell them to do whatever they need to do to keep the lounge at a manageable capacity, or feel free to close entirely if they get overwhelmed."

I followed Cam and the detective down the front steps with Nate at my side.

Detective Sharp hurried into her police SUV and departed, likely eager to get back to the station to interview Will and Kristin.

Nate and I each clapped a hand with the other's and reached around for a one-armed hug.

"Thanks, man," I said. "You saved my life."

He ran his tongue along the inside of his cheek. "Yeah, I did. You owe me *big time*."

I gently pushed his shoulder and waved him off.

And then it was just me and Cam. He led me toward his vehicle and opened the front passenger side door. I climbed inside.

As awkward as it had been interacting with him throughout the investigation, and despite my unfounded fears that he might enact some sort of revenge after I broke up with Chloe, I realized she was right all along.

Cam knew me.

Both concern and relief were written on his face when I sheepishly gazed at him as he buckled in beside me.

"Thanks for all you did for me today." I buckled my seatbelt. "And truly, thanks for everything you've done since I found Brent. I'm sure these past several months since Chloe and I split have been strange for you."

He started to drive and remained silent for what felt like five minutes but was realistically around thirty seconds. "You really broke her heart, Reece."

My heart plunged into my stomach. It was clear how deeply he cared for his younger sister.

"And I'm really sorry. I—"

Cam interrupted. "She had some insanely difficult days when things were fresh. I mean, you completely pulled the rug out from under her." His eyes fixated on the road as he turned onto a side street.

Tempted as I was to interject, I kept quiet so Cam could say his piece.

"I've also watched her grow so much in the last several months. Through it all, she never had a single negative word to say about you. She never expressed any anger about the broken engagement—only disappointment that she wouldn't get to spend the rest of her life with you. But she's moving on, and I'm happy for her."

My voice grew shaky as I tried to respond. "She deserves all the happiness in the world, and I wasn't able to give it to her."

For the first time since I'd brought up the topic, Cam

glanced in my direction to give me a solemn, confirming nod before turning his attention back to the road.

I gulped. "I can explain. I—"

"I don't know what happened between you two, but if she doesn't hold anger in her heart, it'd be unfair for me to."

"Cam, I'm gay," I blurted out.

"Huh?" It was unclear whether he didn't catch what I'd said or if he was processing my revelation.

"I'm gay. I've always struggled with my sexuality and identity, and I thought if I could find a great woman and do what I thought everyone expected of me, I could live happily ever after. And Chloe is an incredible woman. She's so caring and strong and beautiful. I tried to push a very important piece of myself to the side so I could be lucky enough to spend my life with her."

Cam parked the police SUV on the side of the residential street he drove down.

He was speechless.

"When I proposed to Chloe, it wasn't because I wanted to hide part of myself. I proposed because I genuinely wanted to spend forever with her. She was too special of a person to let go." I couldn't stop the tears from flowing out of my eyes and down my face.

Prior to having my life threatened, I would've been embarrassed to cry in front of Cam, but it was impossible to hide in my vulnerable state. "When I broke off our engagement, it wasn't because I was selfish or wanted to live out some repressed fantasy. I did it because I realized it'd be selfish to *stay* in a relationship where I was hiding part of myself. I know ending our engagement was painful for Chloe, but she's been nothing but supportive since I came out to her. She deserves the best of the best, and that's not me."

Cam's lip quivered. He opened his arms and reached across

the center console to pull me into a hug. "I'm so proud of you, man. Thank you for trusting me enough to tell me."

We embraced briefly, and Cam released me with a few firm pats on the back.

"I really do want what's best for Chloe. I know it's probably a lot to process, but thanks for hearing me out."

Cam bit his lower lip. "You may have risked your life to sniff out and confront a murderer, but I'd say coming out is pretty brave, too." He shifted the car into drive. I stared out the passenger side window at the boughs of blooming trees bouncing on the breeze as we continued toward the police station.

Something about what had happened changed me. Of course, I'd been struggling with self-acceptance and coming out for years, but being in a life-threatening situation and facing fear head-on had made me realize how quickly life can change … or even end.

I was ready to share the truth with the people I loved most.

THIRTY

On a Wednesday evening—a couple of weeks after being held at gunpoint—I walked into the vestibule I shared with Heidi. But instead of unlocking the secret bookcase and heading down to Subplot, I strode through the glass front doors of D'Amico's.

In the back corner of the dim restaurant was a large round table for ten, draped with a white tablecloth.

Although I'd originally protested, my parents had organized a birthday dinner for me. I didn't necessarily enjoy being the center of attention, but I couldn't complain about spending an evening with the people I was closest to.

My parents, along with Chloe and Cam, were already seated and in conversation at one side of the table. When I reached them, they paused and each stood up to greet me with a hug and birthday wishes.

"How have you been feeling?" Cam asked once I took a seat to my dad's right.

"The first week after was really rough. I'm still a bit shaken up, but it's letting up a little bit every day. I feel so much lighter knowing I don't have to look over my shoulder."

In the weeks following my run-in with Will, additional

details had come out about the case, which certainly helped me find closure and rest assured that Subplot's reputation wouldn't face any damage.

It turned out Brent had hired Will as his financial advisor after he relocated from Kentucky. In addition to his investments, Brent had inherited a large sum from a family fortune after his parents passed. Will had a discretionary management agreement with Brent, which allowed him to move money and make trades without pre-approval, as long as it resulted in the highest possible yield.

After a while, Brent noticed strange things happening with his finances. He hadn't given Will discretion because he was ignorant about trading. Instead, he felt his time was better spent elsewhere while his money worked for itself. Unfortunately, Will hadn't upheld his fiduciary duty to invest Brent's money according to his best interests.

Instead of reporting his concerns about Will to the authorities right away, Brent did his own research. Brent learned Will owed money to people like Logan. In fact, after catching Will, the authorities figured the scribble on Logan's business card was a hastily written letter *W*. The note read, *W OWES MONEY*, which meant Brent had Will figured out.

Unfortunately, Brent's ego had taken hold. He was intent on exposing Will, blackmailing him, ruining his career, and making his life miserable. It seems Will didn't cope with that very well, so he did the same thing in turn to Kristin.

Because he unfortunately coerced her into committing various crimes after Brent's murder, she had a strong defense to avoid serious legal implications.

My mom gently pushed a breadbasket in my direction. "Help yourself!" Food was certainly her love language.

Over the next several minutes, Nate arrived and sat directly to my right, followed by Lainey and Dante, who sat on the other side of him.

Chloe gestured at the two empty chairs remaining at the table. "Who are we waiting on?"

"Oh, there they are now." My mom pointed at the maître d's stand at the front of the restaurant. "Perfect timing."

Logan and Ava strolled to our table hand-in-hand. It warmed my heart to see they were allowing their relationship to be known. I found it inspiring to see others let love win, despite what naysayers might think.

Though Ava and I had worked together for several shifts since my encounter with Will, I was still haunted by how horribly things could've turned out for one of us if Will's plan to poison Brent hadn't gone according to plan.

Cam had filled me in that Will swiped some of his wife's prescriptions—sedatives—and planted them in the slice of pecan pie Brent ate during the tasting. With alcohol in his system from earlier in the evening and at the tasting, it sped up the process by which his body slowed down. It was no wonder he didn't make it very far after he stormed out of the Lifted Spirits meeting.

Will had meticulously pre-meditated Brent's demise by cutting a faint X in the fatal slice of pie to be sure it was served to the correct target. However, if it'd been served to Ava or me, one of us might not be sitting at the table. I shivered at the thought.

"And who do we have here?" Heidi's voice approached from behind, followed by the squeeze of her ice-cold hands on each of my shoulders. She stood behind and above me with a radiant smile. "I hear we have a birthday in the house. Birthday boy eats for free tonight," she announced to the table before looking down at me. "You order anything you like—drinks, appetizers, dinner, dessert—it's on me."

While Heidi had historically been a pain and a roadblock in my life, I was glad she seemed to be warming up to me and realized I had good intentions.

The evening was filled with laughs and delicious food paired with cabernet sauvignon. I thoroughly enjoyed my favorite meal of all time—lasagna piled high with freshly grated parmesan—while my friends and family told stories and discussed common interests.

After our waitress cleared our main course plates from the table, she returned with a tall slice of cheesecake topped with an elegant raspberry drizzle for each of us.

My slice was decorated with a single candle as the D'Amico's staff and my table sang an enthusiastic "Happy Birthday." It took every ounce of self-control to not slide under the table in embarrassment, though I appreciated my loved ones' caring gesture.

Our waitress then returned with a tray of steaming coffees for those of us who requested it to accompany dessert.

"Before we dig into our cheesecake, I'd like to say something." I first turned to Nate beside me, and he gave me a supportive nod. I slowly rotated my head, looking each person in the eye as I spread my attention around the table until I reached my parents seated to my left. "I can't say thank you enough for coming tonight. As if finding the victim's body a few weeks ago wasn't enough, my run-in with the killer was ..." I struggled to find the words. I clenched my eyes shut as if I could shake the vivid flashback of the gun's barrel aimed between my eyes from my mind. "It was a lot."

"But you were so brave," Logan interjected.

"Thank you." I acknowledged his remark with a bow of my head. "But I also learned bravery can't exist without knowing you have people in your life who love and care about you. It sounds cheesy, but I don't know if I could have faced Will without all of you. There's a certain security and confidence you feel when you know you're loved."

Everyone around the table sat silently, almost as if they anticipated I had more to say.

"And I can't believe I'm about to say this right now—I wasn't sure I ever would. But after everything that's happened, you've all shown me I can't hide any longer. In case you didn't know already, I'm gay. I needed to say it so I can feel free—so I can truly live life to the fullest every single day. After staring death in the eye, I can't take a single breath for granted."

Chloe wiped a tear—which I presumed was one of happiness—from her eye directly across the table from me.

Two arms reached around both of my shoulders.

To my right, Nate nodded his head in support.

And to my left, my father patted my shoulder. "I'm proud of you, buddy."

My mom pushed back her chair and stood up to hug me from behind. I placed a hand on her arm in return. Though she didn't say a word, and despite all the instances in which she'd questioned me about the breakup or pleaded for grandchildren, her embrace made me trust that she loved and supported me no matter what.

I couldn't stop a tear from streaming down my face as I realized that, for the first time in my life, I felt free.

After dinner, I walked back to my apartment alone, comforted in knowing Hope Mills was safe again.

Everyone who'd joined me for dinner offered to give me a ride back to my apartment, but I wanted to savor the crisp air of a beautiful late spring evening without concern that a killer was lurking.

Hope Mills was quiet, except for the sound of the breeze and a train sounding its horn in the distance. I admired the closed cozy shops and dimly-lit restaurants which lined the streets of my hometown's business district as I strolled.

I stared longingly into Ampersand's glowing storefront as I passed by. Peering into its floor-to-ceiling windows, I admired the Mental Health Awareness Month display in front of tables and shelves filled with books. Inside, Julian swept the floors.

I paused for a second on the sidewalk, and I caught his gaze.

I inhaled sharply through my nose and froze for a split second, unsure of what to do. I grinned and gave a small wave.

A slight smirk grew on his face. He waved in return before continuing to sweep, and I continued to walk.

For the rest of my stroll home, I wondered if I'd ever be brave enough to take the next step and ask him out on a date.

"Meooow." Jameson's young, squeaky mew greeted me as soon as I stepped in the door of my dark apartment.

I flicked on the light, delighted by the affectionate orange cat weaving in and out of my legs.

The woman at the animal shelter was right. Jameson was a foster fail for sure.

In the days since I'd found him, I became attached. I couldn't bear the thought of anyone else adopting him, so I'd already called the shelter and asked them to please remove his adoption listing from their website.

Jameson had found his forever home.

I took off my shoes and headed to the kitchen. Jameson skittered behind me, making every effort to lace his body through my legs as I reached for the receipt from Julian, which had been lying on my counter. I picked it up, held it in my hands, and considered how he must've felt when he wrote his number on it. Had he been nervous? Quite possibly. Vulnerable? Maybe. Had he felt brave? Undoubtedly.

I carried the receipt to the couch, and Jameson curled up on my lap as soon as I sat down. He purred as I scratched behind his ears and under his chin.

In that moment, I realized how much time and energy I'd spent on my breakup with Chloe. I'd been so focused on the door closing behind me, and it influenced every move I made—from starting my business to my fear of coming out.

But after being surrounded by my loved ones at dinner, I was finally able to turn around and see the door opening in front of me.

I slid my phone out of my pocket and began to type the numbers written in blue ink at the bottom of the receipt.

While I'd been fixated for so long on one chapter ending, I finally felt free enough to embrace the chapter which was about to begin.

Life was too short to live in the shadows.

Dear reader,

Thank you for taking the time to read *Whiskey Business*. I hope you found a joyful escape in the town of Hope Mills and within the cozy walls of Subplot.

If you'd like to receive access to giveaways, cocktail and mocktail recipes, updates about upcoming books, behind-the-scenes content, short stories, and sneak peeks at what's to come, please sign up for my newsletter. I have lots to share!

www.adrianandover.com/newsletter

I'd also be endlessly grateful if you took the time to leave an honest review wherever you buy books or track your reading. Reviews go a long way in helping others find their way to my story, which means the world to me.

Also, check out my social media links on the next page so we can stay connected. One of my favorite parts about writing is the community we can share, connected by our love for stories.

I wish you love and peace. Be kind to yourself, and stay hydrated!

Sincerely,
Adrian

STAY IN TOUCH WITH ME

Visit my website:

www.adrianandover.com

Let's connect on social media:

instagram.com/adrianandover

facebook.com/adrianandover

threads.com/@adrianandover

bsky.app/profile/adrianandover.com

youtube.com/@adrianandover

ACKNOWLEDGMENTS

Long before I sat down to write a novel of my own, I always marveled over the Acknowledgements in my favorite books and wondered how an author could possibly have so many people to thank.

Now that I'm publishing my debut, I've learned firsthand that it truly takes a community to bring a book to life. I have many people to thank, and I am so grateful for every person who has played a role in this journey.

First and foremost, I must thank the incredible family and friends in my life. I don't think I would've had the courage and belief in myself to write without your love and support in all I do. My love and gratitude for you is boundless.

Major thanks are in order for Ellie Alexander, my teacher and mentor. Also—sending a huge shoutout to my classmates in Ellie's Author Academy. Your support, answers to my many questions and discussion topics, and the sense of community you all offered helped guide me along this journey.

I have so much gratitude for my Inky Fingers critique group —Paula Charles, Annie McEwen, Leah Dobrinska, Christina Romeril, Kara Lacey, and J.R. Lancaster. You all welcomed me in as the only unpublished author in the group, and you believed in me every step of the way. Your feedback on my early draft was critical to the shape this story took.

My beta readers Kat Webb, Marcus Gaetano, and Emily Stubbs provided encouraging and helpful feedback on an earlier draft as well. Thanks to your feedback on what was and wasn't working, I was able to craft a story I feel so proud of. Thank you for taking a chance on me and volunteering to read this unknown author's story.

Korina Moss, thank you for your thoughtful and detailed developmental feedback. Your love of mysteries is palpable, and I am grateful for your belief in this story.

I met Eryn Scott and Angela M. Sanders at the Ashland Mystery Festival in 2024. Neither of them knew I existed when I met them, yet they each offered to spend hours with me to share their expertise on publishing as well as their encouragement.

Kelly Shermer, thank you for driving from Bend to Portland while I sat silently in the passenger seat, typing away as I planned for this book's publication. You saw my spark turn into a fire, and I appreciate your support.

If you picked up this book because of its stunning cover, Dawn Adams is responsible. I am still in awe every time I look at it. She truly brought my vision for Subplot to life.

Thanks to my editor Bryn Donovan and proofreader Ericka Turnbull. Your attention to detail and encouraging feedback helped me tidy up the story and tighten up the prose.

To the mystery community—I am blown away by the support, friendliness, and warmth this amazing group of readers and writers offers. I never could've imagined the friendships I've made, both online and in-person. *That* is the power of stories. Our love for reading connects us, and I will be forever thankful for you.

And to you, dear reader. Thank you for picking up this book from a debut author. I hope you found a piece of yourself in this story.

ABOUT THE AUTHOR

Adrian Andover is the author of *Whiskey Business*, his debut novel and the first entry in the Mixology Lounge Mysteries series.

When he's not reading, writing, revising, or publishing a story, he enjoys long walks, attending live music events, spending time with friends, and tasting new craft cocktails around his chosen hometown of Asbury Park, NJ.